MY STORY
HIGHWAY GIRL

VALERIE WILDING

SCHOLASTIC

For Ed and Sue, for all the fun.
Thank you, please!

While the events described and some of the characters in this book may be based on actual historical events and real people, Susannah Makepeace is a fictional character, created by the author, and her diary is a work of fiction.

Scholastic Children's Books,
Euston House, 24 Eversholt Street,
London NW1 1DB, UK

A division of Scholastic Ltd
London ~ New York ~ Toronto ~ Sydney ~ Auckland
Mexico City ~ New Delhi ~ Hong Kong

First published in the UK by Scholastic Ltd, 2009
This edition published by Scholastic Ltd, 2015

ISBN 978 1407 15660 6

Typeset by M Rules
Printed and bound in the UK by CPI Group (UK) Ltd, Croydon, CR0 4YY

2 4 6 8 10 9 7 5 3 1

Papers used by Scholastic Children's Books are made from woods grown in sustainable forests.

www.scholastic.co.uk

February 6th, 1670

I am excited; I am afraid. I am sad, yet I am glad. And how shocked Mama would be if she knew that I have just altered a pair of my brother's breeches to fit me!

For tonight, under cover of darkness, Dominic and I must leave our little home, forever. My only comfort is that I shall be taking Jack with me. He is the dearest little dog, and I could not bear to be parted from him. I have lost too much. First Father dying, after suffering so much from the wounds he received from the Roundheads in the ghastly war against our king's Cavaliers. At least he lived to see Charles II restored to the throne. And now, ten years on, our poor dear mother has passed away, too.

It was a sad little funeral, for there are so few people here in Lustleigh, on the edge of Dartmoor. It's a pretty village, but tiny. Beside the open grave, Dominic took my chilled hand and spoke for us both.

"Mama," he said, "when Father died and left us in debt, you bravely took charge of our little family, selling our house and bringing us to the cottage – our little haven – which we've loved so much."

At this point, I noticed our landlord cast a glance at Dominic. It was not kindly meant, that was clear.

"Mama," Dominic continued, "you are now in heaven. Watch over Susannah and me. We will always cherish your memory, and we will make you proud of us."

Dominic must know that she was already proud of him, for we could not have afforded the rent without his help. As soon as he was old enough, he had travelled to London, to work for a merchant acquaintance of Father's, and sent us whatever money he could spare. It was never enough – we were constantly selling bits and pieces of our possessions in order to eat.

But how brave, to go alone to a big city! London is a hundred times the size of Exeter, he told us, though that cannot be. Exeter, which I have twice visited, makes me dizzy!

But Dominic was always ready for adventure. And that's why I feel such fear and sadness today. For he is not to return to London to work. He has a plan, and it does not include me.

I hear his horse. Dominic has been on a difficult errand.

Later

Dominic collapsed on to the settle, looking cold and exhausted.

"That's it, Susannah," he said. "I've sold everything. I have paid every bill I can, but we still have some creditors who remain unpaid."

"Including our landlord."

Dominic nodded. "Him, of course. So!" He shrugged. "The Makepeace family – what's left of us – must shift the best they can."

"We go tonight?"

"Tonight." He picked up the only book we possess, the Makepeace family Bible, and clutched it to his chest. "Though it hurts so much to run, Su."

"Dearest Dominic, you will make it all right, one day. You will, I know it."

He squeezed my arm. "I'm glad you have faith in me. I wish our landlord had. Twenty days to pay everything we owe him."

"It's not enough."

"And that's why we must disappear tonight." Dominic

slumped, his head in his hands. "Oh, Su, the shame of it! Doing this goes against all our upbringing, against all the values we Makepeaces hold dear."

I knelt and looked up into his eyes. "But it's right, isn't it? What we're doing is right?" I needed reassurance. I wish, how I wish I could be strong, but I'm not.

He nodded slowly. "It's the only way."

We're going a week before the twenty days are up; that makes it less likely that our flight will be suspected. Only one person has our confidence, and that is Ned Allin, who has been with us for years, and has stuck with us through good times and bad. Mama took pity on him when his father died, because he has one leg much shorter and thinner than the other, and is much laughed at by the village boys. He cannot fight them because his arm, on the same side as the bad leg, is weak. People would not hire him, but he is a good worker, and used to look after our horses and stables. Since Father died, and we fell on hard times, Ned has cared for Dominic's horse, Moonbeam, as well as our cow and the pig we'd been fattening. He is to help us tonight.

In a moment Dominic and I will take a last posy of flowers to Mama's grave. And then we'll eat some of our bread and cheese, and wrap the rest together with a few slightly wrinkled apples for our journey. This will probably be our last meal together. My next proper meal will be with

Sir Roger de Gracy and his family. At the moment, they are nothing to me, being but distant cousins, but soon I expect to know them almost as well as I knew my own mother. For they have kindly extended an invitation to us, to share their home, Gracy Park, in Somerset.

I have accepted, but Dominic would not. He says he'd rather die than accept charity. He is to accompany me as far as Exeter and then we will begin our new lives. Our – oh, I can scarcely bear to write this – our new, separate lives.

My beloved brother cannot bear the thought that we are skulking off in secret. It is dishonourable. He vows that he will go away and make his fortune, and one day he will return to clear our debts and make everything all right again. I must support him in this adventure, but it breaks my heart that he will be so far from me.

For Dominic is going to America.

February 7th (early hours)

What a night this has been! During the afternoon, Ned arrived on his ancient bay mare, which I was to ride to the coaching inn at the crossroads, five miles away. He looked so surprised – and shocked – when he saw me, for

I'd already changed into Dominic's breeches and his old doublet and coat, ready for our night ride. I wore riding boots, too, and a high felt hat.

Ned loaded my two boxes and my woollen bag on to our old handcart. He was to push that to a small copse beside the coaching inn, where we'd meet. He doesn't make fast progress, and preferred to start out early so that he might travel in daylight. He fears the darkness.

"Ned," said Dominic, "you will keep our animals—"

"Oh, not Jack!" I cried.

Dominic smiled. "Of course not Jack," he said. "Ned will take Jack to meet us at the coaching inn, won't you, Ned?"

"I will, Mistress Susannah, never fear," said Ned. "I know how you loves that little dog."

"But our cow and the pig," said Dominic, "they are to be yours, Ned, for you have been our one true friend through all our hardship."

Ned couldn't speak. He reached up and rubbed his old horse's face so fast that she started back in surprise.

I kissed my dear Jack and promised to be with him shortly, and off Ned went, trundling along the lane on the start of his long walk to the inn. I watched him go, his right shoulder dipping with every step. He took with him everything I own and hold dear, apart from my brother.

There was little to do but wait. When darkness fell, I sat

on the window seat and gazed at the stars. Dominic dozed, and I must have done, too, because I jumped, startled, when he said, "Time to get ready, Su."

Dressed in Mama's dark cloak, my hair pinned up, and with Dominic's hat pulled low, I stood before him. He smiled.

"You will pass for a lad," he said. "A little lad, 'tis true, but a lad all the same."

We went outside and closed the door for the last time. I noticed that Dominic limped a little, but he hushed me when I asked.

Once mounted, there was nothing to do but say a whispered farewell to our home and to leave Lustleigh. At first it felt strange to ride astride, as I used to do as a small child. Eventually Mama taught me to ride side-saddle. She said a lady should always be a lady, whether alone or in company, and I followed her example. But I was a good rider from the beginning, so I soon felt at home riding astride again.

Though cold, the night was still and damp. I sniffed the soft Devon air and a sudden feeling of being free and alive almost overwhelmed me. I urged the old mare to a trot, which she reluctantly managed, but Dominic moved forward and grasped my rein.

"Susannah, stay by my side," he warned. "We probably wouldn't be recognized, even if it's known that we've fled, because people would expect a man and a girl, but we mustn't take chances. If we meet anyone, I will speak. Do you understand?"

"Yes, brother," I said. I knew he was nervous, because he kept nibbling his lower lip – something he's done all his life when agitated or afraid.

"It can be dangerous to ride at night, anyway," he said.

As he spoke, the moon disappeared behind a cloud, and my horse stumbled. I whimpered in fear.

"Don't worry, Su," he said. "We'll be all right."

"What about highwaymen?"

"This road is too little travelled," he replied. "There are no rich pickings for highwaymen here, so why should we encounter one?"

"But if we did, all our money would be stolen."

He chuckled. "I thought of that. I have a small pouch at my belt, see? It has a few coins inside. The rest of our money, such as it is, is safely tucked inside my boots."

So that was why he limped!

The moon reappeared, and I saw that we were on an open, deeply rutted track, lined by woodland. And we were approaching a small hamlet – just a few cottages.

Without warning, a horse and rider stepped out of the trees and turned to face us head on. A pistol pointed directly at us. It seemed as if it pointed at my heart.

My stomach tumbled over.

"Stand!" said the masked rider.

We pulled up, and Dominic leaned over to take my rein. "Pull your hat lower," he hissed.

In terror, I obeyed.

The highwayman – for that was what he was – held out a gloved hand. "Your money!" he barked.

Dominic's voice shook when he spoke. "We have little money. This is all my brother and I have between us." He pulled the pouch from his belt and approached the robber, his head held high. At that moment, I was proud that he showed no fear, though I knew he was very afraid.

The highwayman moved towards him. When their horses were alongside each other, he stopped. All the time he pointed the pistol at Dominic. Leaning forward, he reached for the pouch of coins.

As my brave brother held it out, the highwayman gave a start. He stared directly at Dominic for a long moment, then said, "God go with you. I shall not rob you." With that, he turned his horse's head and rode back into the trees, as silently as he had come.

He was gone. The danger was past. For at least a minute, we stared at the spot from where he'd vanished, then turned to look at each other. Was my face as pale as Dominic's? His only colour was a smudge of blood where he'd bitten his lip. I was aware of my heart thudding.

"Why did—" I began, but Dominic stopped me.

"Hush, Su. Let's be gone from here." He glanced up at the sky. "The clouds will soon cover the moon again, and we have a way to go yet."

I felt confused. Why had the highwayman let us go without taking our money? The change in him came about when he was close to my brother. I suddenly realized why.

"Dominic! He recognized you! Oh, mercy, the highwayman must have been someone we know!"

"I think you're right, Su. Come on. A little faster, if you can get that old nag to make an effort."

I managed to coax the mare into a lumbering canter, and we were soon through the woodland and its hidden dangers. Once we'd slowed, Dominic came alongside so we could whisper.

"But if he knows you," I said, "he must know our situation, and he must realize what we're doing. He will realize we're running away. If he tells—"

"Hush, sister. He will not tell anyone. If he meant us harm, he would have robbed us. Remember his words? 'God go with you.' He means us no harm."

We rode along quietly. It wasn't much further to the inn. I pondered on our frightening experience, and it dawned on me that if the highwayman had known us, then we must know him! But surely not! We don't know any criminals.

I thought of all the people we knew. Could one of them – a simple farmer, or a blacksmith perhaps – take to the

highway by night and become a robber? Lord knows, m
of them are poor enough. But are they poor enough to take the risk? Because one thing is certain, the penalty for highway robbery is death.

At long last, the inn came in sight. The coach stood in the courtyard, the driver asleep on his seat. Just past the main buildings, set well back from the road, was a large dilapidated barn. Beyond that was a copse of stunted oak trees, and that's where we headed. Once out of sight of the road, Dominic whistled, long and low. There was an answering whistle, then the sound of rapid movement through the undergrowth.

"Dominic! What is it? It's an animal!"

Before he could reply, a bundle of white fur leapt at my knees.

"Jack! My Jack!"

Ned appeared next. "He's right glad to see you, Mistress Susannah!" he said with a grin.

"And I him! Thank you!"

"You must be frozen, Ned," said Dominic. "Did you reserve a room for us to wait in?"

"That I did," said Ned. "The boxes are already aboard."

"And my bag?" I asked. "Do you have my woollen bag?"

"It's on the cart still, just over yonder," said Ned.

He limped away to fetch it, and returned a moment later. His leg must have ached badly after his long walk.

"I'll go back and wait by the cart, Mistress Susannah," he said, "while you, um, do what's necessary."

"I daren't leave you, Su," said Dominic. "I will turn my back."

I'll never forget the next few minutes, when I had to change my clothes behind a holly bush in the middle of a dark wood, at night, with my brother standing not ten feet away, and another young man just out of sight. I remember thinking, "Oh my, whatever have we come to, that I must do this?"

But soon I was dressed and decent. Gone was the "little lad", and here once more was Mistress Susannah Makepeace.

I returned the mare to Ned, with my grateful thanks, and began to say farewell. But he shook his head.

"I'll say my goodbye in the morning, when you leave, Mistress."

"But where will you sleep in the meantime?"

"Here," he said. "Master Dominic said I can keep the cart. And I must see the horses stabled. That'll warm me up! But first I'll show you your room, to save disturbing the inn host. He's a surly, grumpy fellow when awake. I'd hate to rouse him from his bed."

My brother took my arm. "Come, Su," he said. "We must sleep a little."

"Wait." I picked up Jack. He never barks when he's in my arms.

Ned led us to the inn, opened a little side door and showed us to our room. It was very poor, and very stuffy. I threw the window open before bidding Ned goodnight. I was embarrassed then to have to ask Dominic to leave the room for a few minutes. I desperately needed to use the chamber pot which I was glad to find beneath the bed.

Now all is quiet, except for Dominic, who snores softly on the floor, wrapped in a moth-eaten wool rug, which I'm sure is probably flea-ridden, too.

Dawn

I have been unable to sleep, and not just because of being nibbled by fleas! Twice I have taken out the letter from Sir Roger de Gracy, in which he invites us to Gracy Park. I am to spend the night in another inn at Honiton, and the de Gracy carriage is being sent to meet me the next morning. I hope it will not be late. I fear having to wait alone in a strange place.

Alone. What a frightening word that is. Today, when I have said farewell to Dominic, I will be alone.

But I have my new family to go to. For though very distant, they are family. There's a daughter who is, I believe, little more than a couple of years older than me. I am sure we will become great friends.

I will be happy there. I will. I must, for it will be a long time, I know, before Dominic returns. And then – oh, then! He will be finely dressed and will have found a home for us and settled all our debts. And he'll come to claim me, and we'll live a sparkling life, and I will marry well and have a whole flock of children, who will love me and follow me round like so many lambs, and I'll never be alone again.

February 8th (morning)

I am grateful that the landlord of the coaching inn, here in Honiton, has such a gentle wife. She has given me this corner, out of the way of prying eyes, to wait in until the carriage comes from Gracy Park. I have spent a sleepless night, alone and in such misery. Now, until I am collected, I have time to write about our separation, but I can barely see the letters I form, for my eyes constantly swim with tears.

When Dominic put me in the coach yesterday morning, he told me he would ride alongside for a few miles until, past Exeter, he was to turn north to head for Taunton and Bristol, while I continued to Honiton. I was happy and I was upset, all at once. Glad that I would be with him a while longer, and upset because I had hardened myself to say farewell and would have to do it all over again.

We had a surprise in store which took my mind off my sadness for a few minutes. In the yard Ned stood as straight as he could, with Dominic's horse, Moonbeam, and his own mare ready, brushed and shining. He would not leave my brother's side, and when Dominic asked why he did not start for home, Ned replied, "What home have I got? You and Mistress Susannah are my only friends – as I am yours. I'll go with you, Master Dominic, to the new world – if you'll have me, that is, begging your pardon."

Dominic put both hands on Ned's shoulders. "I will, and gladly," he said. "We'll make our way together, and share whatever we meet, both good and ill."

Ned held out a handful of coins. "I've sold the cart. The cow and the pig can graze until people realize we're gone."

Dominic grinned. "Then we—"

But he was interrupted by shouts. The coach was laden and ready to go. Two passengers were already aboard.

"To horse, Ned!" cried Dominic.

I was glad to see him in such high spirits. Having a companion with him has changed his view of the journey, there's no doubt about that! I was also glad to be leaving the inn. We were too close to home. There was still a chance that someone might have missed us already, and would come looking for us. Dominic helped me climb aboard, and handed Jack to me. I sat next to a large, jolly-faced woman, who did not mind my little dog in the least. A thin man opposite – so bony I could have cut cheese with his cheekbones – did not look my way once.

And we were off! I was much comforted that whenever the way was wide enough, Dominic, and sometimes Ned, rode alongside, leaned down and doffed their hats. It made me feel such a lady!

We stopped at Exeter, and everyone went into the inn, some to eat and some, like me, to find a maidservant and ask directions to a room where I might take care of my needs. Then Dominic, Ned and I sat by the fire, shared our food and drank some very good ale. Dominic gave me some money and told me to hide it in my chemise.

"You will have need of it, Su," he said. "I don't like to think of you penniless." He smiled, but his front teeth nibbled at his lower lip. "Next time I give you money, my dearest sister, it will be gold! You'll see!"

Some new passengers boarded, and soon we were on our way again. The road was dry and the coach sped along. All too soon, Dominic called, "The way parts at the brow of the hill, Su. We must now say farewell."

"No!" I cried. "Not so quickly! Stop the coach. Oh, please stop the coach! I must hug you, just one last time. Please, Dominic!"

I was appalled to see his face flush, and his eyes fill. I leaned out of the window, shouting, "Driver, stop! For pity's sake, stop!"

The coach slowed and clattered to a halt. There was much cursing from the front and a gruff snort from the bony man. I clambered out. Poor Jack became entangled in my skirts and tumbled to the ground.

I hurled myself into Dominic's arms. Behind me the thin man and the coachmen moaned and grumbled. "Here of all places," I heard, and, "'Tis not fit for a lady's eyes," and, "It do stink, too."

Only after I'd had the heartbreaking experience of waving my brother and friend a last goodbye and watching them disappear into a small wood down the lane to the left, did I turn and take in my surroundings.

I screamed in horror. My cries set Jack barking. I scooped him up and scrambled back into the coach. As we drew away I looked once more at the hideous object which had frightened me so. It was a gibbet: a metal cage that held the rotting remains of what had once been a man.

"Highwayman," said the big woman. "Got what he deserved, no doubt, when they hanged him, but does any soul deserve to be left for the birds to peck out his eyes, I wonder?"

Against my will, I recalled the robber who held us up – was it only the night before? This stinking, gibbeted corpse had once been a living, breathing man like him. If ever there was a warning to stay on the straight and narrow path of goodness, that was it.

And then I thought of how Dominic and I have strayed from that path. And I wept.

Remembering our parting brings unwanted tears to my eyes once more. But I am being called! The carriage from Gracy Park must be here!

February 9th, at Gracy Park

Lady Anne sent a footman to escort me to church this morning, which was most kind, but I declined. I told the footman to explain that I need to recover from my experiences of the last few days, and I'm sure they will understand.

Now, listening to the sound of church bells and birdsong, I sit by my little open window, for the weather is still, and this cottage is sheltered. I breathe in soft, clear air, and write at a pretty octagonal pear-wood table. I don't have the window open in order to admire the view, lovely though it is, but to try to stay awake. I am so tired after yesterday's journey, but I want to write down my experiences before I forget them. When Dominic returns, it will amuse him to read this and to know how I have fared.

As the landlord's good wife took me out to the carriage yesterday, I felt there had been some mistake. With my parents, I travelled in carriages many times, especially in our own modest one, but I had never been in one as grand as this! I do not know which shone more – horses or carriage!

A footman assisted me in, passed Jack to me, and took care of my boxes. I kept my woollen bag with me. I was afraid that it might be dropped, or perhaps fall, and all would see the breeches and man's hat which were within!

The carriage was so much more comfortable than the coach but, of course, the main difference was that I was alone, apart from Jack.

At first I relaxed and enjoyed my velvet and silken surroundings, but after a while I began to feel sick with all the swaying. I must have dozed a little, but woke suddenly with the feeling that something was wrong. Then I realized. We were stationary. I looked out to ask what was amiss, but the carriage driver came to my door and assured me that all was well.

"We wait awhile in this village for other travellers," he said. "See, Mistress Makepeace? There are others waiting too."

Indeed there were. "Why do we wait?" I asked.

"There's safety in numbers." He waved his whip, indicating the long, steadily sloping hill. "And 'tis hard to make speed on an upward climb such as that. When carriages and coaches go slowly, well, that's the time they're most in danger."

"Danger?" I had thought I was safe at last. "Danger from what?"

"From highwaymen, Mistress," he replied. "If a highwayman should attack on a hill such as that, he'd know we couldn't pick up speed and get away, and he'd know he could escape downhill and vanish like a fox into a forest."

"Mercy!"

He smiled. "Don't be afraid, Mistress. You'll be well protected."

"And indeed, I have nothing worth stealing," I said, attempting a shaky smile.

He opened the carriage door. "Most passengers like to wait in the inn yonder." He pointed to a pretty, low building just across a narrow stream where ducks bobbed and squabbled. "'Tis clean enough, and they provide good food to hungry travellers."

"Oh." I shrank back into my seat. "I, um, I—"

Bless the man, for he seemed to sense my predicament. "I am instructed to bear all expenses on your behalf, Mistress," he said. "You go in, and have something to eat and drink, and tell Old Joan I'll settle your account. Sir Roger has provided," he went on as I began to protest.

I was glad to rest inside, and Old Joan – it must have been she, for she was at least forty – knew how to treat a lady, for she took me straight to a little room at the top of her narrow stairs, and said, "Here you may refresh yourself in private, m'lady. Your dinner will be ready directly."

I was most relieved to use the facilities inside the room,

and returned downstairs shortly, where I ate a good meal of a beef pasty and hot gravy.

Old Joan gave Jack a bone with much meat on it. He took it outside, as he has been trained to do, and lay on the step in the sunshine, gnawing away happily. I felt much better.

Soon, the carriage driver, who is called Luke, appeared in the doorway. He removed his hat. "Pardon me, Mistress Makepeace, but we must leave now."

I thanked him, called Jack, and went back to the carriage. Luke must have settled Old Joan's account, for she came out to wave us off.

Aside from us, the group of travellers consisted of a carriage-and-four, two carters, a farmwife mounted on a mule, three churchmen on horseback and another on a jittery-looking donkey. There was also a pony pulling a strange-looking contraption that looked as if someone had created a small carriage out of an old cart, like ours.

Thoughts of our cart brought a wave of melancholy, which I quickly dismissed. For goodness' sake, Susannah, I thought, take hold of your spirits and stop being such a softling.

I'd clearly eaten too much, as I felt queasy as soon as we crested the hill. I tried to sleep a little, but when I closed my eyes it felt as if the world moved beneath me. I think it must be how sailors feel on a ship on the ocean. Poor Dominic and Ned.

I did drift, a little, and came to when I felt Jack jump up beside me. Bless him, he had made a dreadful mess on the floor with his bone. I quickly crouched down to pick up the scraps that remained, and flung them through the window.

After another hour, I sensed the horses had picked up speed. I feared there might be trouble – perhaps a hold-up. A carriage like Sir Roger de Gracy's would be a sure target for a highwayman. I peeped out of the window.

What a sight! An elegant, stone house lying low amid great sweeps of grass, glowing golden in the late afternoon sunshine.

I shouted to Luke. "Is this—?" but the wind took my breath away.

"Ay, 'tis Gracy Park, Mistress," he called back.

My new home, I thought, and I marvelled at my good fortune.

Sir Roger and Lady Anne de Gracy actually came out to meet me, with three of their servants. The warmth of their greeting almost overwhelmed me.

"Come in, my dear, and welcome," said Lady Anne, and she kissed my cheek.

"Welcome indeed," said Sir Roger. "We are delighted to meet you, cousin Susannah."

They seemed a little nonplussed by my lack of baggage, but I thought it best to be honest.

"I have few possessions now," I said, then in case they thought I was going to beg from them, "but I have more than enough for my needs."

Both smiled, but I felt that, at that moment, they felt differently about me.

Lady Anne noticed Jack for the first time. Bless him, his ears and tail stood up as if a maid had starched them!

"It is your dog?" asked Lady Anne.

"Yes. His name is Jack," I said.

"How charming." Her fixed smile spoke differently.

Sir Roger bade me come inside. I thought it odd that my baggage had not been removed from the carriage, but said nothing.

Jack was exploring the carriage wheels and I knew what he was about to do, so I called him. "Come, Jack."

But Lady Anne stood in the doorway. "No, no, cousin Susannah. He cannot come into the house. My sweet Juliana has a fear of dogs, and will become ill if one comes near."

"Oh, but—"

Luke stepped forward and picked Jack up. "Begging your pardon, m'lady," he said to Lady Anne, "I'll look after the little dog in the coach house."

I felt panic rising, "But I cannot—"

"Come, my dear," said Sir Roger. "Take some refreshment, and then you can come back for your little dog. Luke will take great care of it, I promise."

I felt Sir Roger understood my fear of being parted from Jack. "He is all I have," I explained, as we went into the hall.

Lady Anne sent a maid scurrying for food and drink.

"But you have your brother, too," she said, showing me to a seat at a small table. "Is he far behind you? We thought you would come together, but perhaps he prefers to—"

"Lady Anne, Sir Roger... My brother is not to come to Gracy Park."

They looked mystified.

"He has gone to America," I said. "To make his fortune," I added, taking advantage of them being stunned into silence. "He will return one day, and then I will not be obliged to take advantage of your kindness and generosity any longer."

I am so angry with myself, because what did I do then but burst into tears. It clearly embarrassed them, because they just sat there, as if I wasn't even in the room. Lady Anne examined the lace at her wrist, and Sir Roger cleared his throat. Twice. "Errk, hmm."

When I'd pulled myself together, Lady Anne noticed me again and said, "I'll tell the maids to prepare a room for you."

I was taken aback. They seemed to have expected both Dominic and me. Why, then, were rooms not prepared for us? I think my jaw dropped, for Lady Anne quickly explained. "We thought you and your brother might care to set up home in a cottage in Gracy Park. It is a good-sized one, and we thought – well, we thought you would feel more independent." She hesitated. "We mean well, dear cousin. Life has been difficult for you, and we do not want you to feel as if you are a poor relation, living off – well, off richer ones. D'you see?"

But that's exactly how I do feel.

Later

My new maid, Bid, has just been in to see me with a pile of linen, and she interrupted my writing.

"Do you read, Bid?" I asked.

She laughed. "No, Mistress Makepeace! I can't do nothing clever."

Good. It means I may safely leave my diary on the octagonal table. But it also means I cannot ask her if I spell her name correctly. Bid or Bidd? Or even Bydd? I do not know.

I am relieved to be settled here in Keeper's Cottage. After Lady Anne and Sir Roger had got over their shock at me being on my own, there was a flurry of maids and whispered instructions, and all my protests were brushed aside. I have good ears and it soon became plain that arrangements were going ahead to prepare a room for me in the house. And so it proved.

"Cousin Susannah," said Lady Anne, "you are on your

own! We cannot let you live alone. You must live in this house. And if you wish, you may take your meals with us and—"

"And Jack?"

"Jack?"

"My dog. He would be with me?"

Lady Anne became flustered. "Heavens, no! My sweet Juliana couldn't tolerate an animal in the house. Gracious, no."

Sir Roger patted my shoulder. "You will soon get used to living without the dog, my dear. It can live in the stables. The servants will feed it and groom it and whatnot."

This was too much! After all I'd been through! "*He!*" I blurted. "Jack is a he, not an it."

Sir Roger stepped back, eyebrows raised, and with an expression of distaste. "Wife, you deal with this," he said to Lady Anne. "Young girls nowadays ... don't know what the world's coming to..." He wandered from the room.

I felt dreadful. How could I be so impertinent to these good people? "I apologize, Lady Anne," I said, "but I have lost so much – I cannot be parted from Jack."

She shrugged. "Then there is no choice. You will live in Keeper's Cottage. I shall send Bid to be with you."

"Bid?"

"A maid. She is of little enough use to us. She needs to be chivvied the whole time. If there are only two of you in the cottage, you will be well placed to keep a close eye on her."

I took a deep breath. It was going to be all right. Odd! Only an hour before I had expected to live in the house. Then when the idea of the cottage was dangled before me, I couldn't think of anything more desirable than to live alone. "I thank you, Lady Anne," I said. "May I go to Keeper's Cottage, to settle in before night falls?"

"Certainly not, my dear," she replied. "You will stay and sup with us, then one of the footmen will light you to your new home. In the meantime, Bid can go and unpack your boxes and make sure that all is prepared for you. Why not take a walk around the park until supper time? There is no wind and the snowdrops are lovely. You have an hour."

I would sooner have changed my clothes and washed my face, but a walk meant a chance to be with Jack and to check he'd be looked after while I ate.

A footman called Joseph, who is Luke's son, showed me to the coach house, where I found Jack looking perfectly happy.

"Oh, Luke, thank you!" I said, hugging my little treasure. "But may I return with Jack in an hour? I'm to sup with the family, and then a footman – Joseph, I suppose – will light my way to Keeper's Cottage. I will collect Jack when I leave."

'Keeper's Cottage?' Luke's eyes widened. "Do you mean Keeper's Cottage down by the front gates?"

"I suppose so."

"You won't be staying there alone, will 'ee, Mistress?"

"No, I won't," I said, "though I am not afraid to be alone. Nor am I frightened of the dark, and I'm sure there will be candles."

"Who will be living there, along of 'ee?" he asked.

"I don't know if I got the name right," I said. "Lady Anne mentioned someone called … Bid."

"Bid?" he said. "Are you telling me Bid is going to stay with you? She won't like that. No, she won't."

I felt most offended. "How can you know if she'll like it? She's never met me. Come along, Jack. Let's go and look at the wretched snowdrops."

I did my best to sweep out of the coach house, but Luke hurried after me. "No, no, Mistress, I didn't mean that. Bid will like *you*, I've no doubt. Anybody would like you."

I folded my arms. "Then what did you mean?"

He opened his mouth to speak, but was interrupted by a high, thin voice.

"Mistress Susannah Makepeace?"

I turned to see a girl, a little taller than myself, and a great deal better-dressed. I went to her. "Yes, I am Susannah Makepeace."

"I am glad to meet you," said the girl, who had thin, pale lips and wide, piercing ice-blue eyes. Her fur-lined cloak, the colour of ripe wheat, almost matched the curls clustered at each side of her face. "I am—" She looked past me. "Aaaaagh!" she screeched. "What is that?"

I had a job to control myself. First Jack was an "it", and now he was a "that".

"He is my dog – Jack," I said.

"Ugh! Take it away, Luke," she ordered. Then she spun round and stalked away.

I waited.

She looked back. "Well, come then. Walk with me."

I handed Jack to Luke, whose mouth twitched, I swear it did. Then I followed Juliana. For I was sure that this snapdragon, whom I'd looked forward to meeting, and perhaps to becoming friends with, was my distant cousin, Juliana de Gracy.

As we walked, I was treated to a monologue about Juliana. Juliana's dancing, Juliana's wardrobe, Juliana's embroidery skills, Juliana's tapestry designs, Juliana's artistic talent, Juliana's musical ear (which I wanted to box) and more and more of her favourite subject Juliana. Not once did she ask about me.

A surprise awaited me at the supper table. Juliana's brother, Godfrey, a boy of about eleven, joined us. He is the most delightful child – his face is open and fresh, and when he smiles, his eyes do, too. And he smiles often.

Lady Anne and Juliana kept the conversation going – non-stop. Sir Roger applied himself to his wine and his plate, and seldom spoke. Few words were addressed to me, and I found myself trying to smother my yawns. Once I had to clench my teeth really hard to stop my mouth opening wide, and I know my top lip curled as if I smelled a nasty smell. I glanced up. Godfrey was watching me, and he gave me a wicked little smile. I shall like Godfrey.

Once supper was over, Sir Roger spoke at last. "Well, cousin Susannah, your maid will have prepared your new home, so I will call a man to light your way. You will be pleased to take your dog, no doubt."

"Dog?" said Godfrey, looking from me to his father and back again. "You have a dog? Really?"

"She does indeed," said Juliana. "And it will stay at Keeper's Cottage."

Godfrey stared. "Cousin Susannah's going to live in Keeper's Cottage?"

Lady Anne said firmly, "She is. It is her choice."

Godfrey looked at me with respect. "Zooks!" he said, and was rewarded with a cuff on the side of the head for his language.

As they bade me goodnight, Lady Anne said, "If you are bothered by … by anything at Keeper's Cottage, you will tell me, won't you? You do not need to stay there."

I promised I would, and reassured her that I would be fine.

And so here I sit at the octagonal table. And I look out

and wonder, how does my brother fare? How long will it be until we meet again? I pray that I will have the patience to wait, for I know it may be years, and I am not the most patient of girls.

February 10th

What a night! I began to think Bid must be completely mad!

I was fast asleep in my large, very comfortable bed, when she burst in, clutching a lit candle stump, and terrifying both me and Jack.

"Mistress, please let me sleep along o' you."

"Bid, whatever is the matter?" I struggled to collect my wits.

"I'll curl up on the floor, I will, you won't know I'm here!"

I wasn't going to let her curl up anywhere until I'd found out what was wrong.

"I'm scared I might see the keeper," she blubbered.

"What keeper?"

"Him! The keeper as lived here. This be Keeper's Cottage."

I couldn't understand a word she said, but she was clearly

terrified, so I threw back my bedcovers and patted the mattress. "Come, rest here for a moment and tell me what is the trouble." In truth, I was beginning to get jittery myself.

Bid didn't need to be asked twice. She leapt into the bed and pulled the coverlet over her eyes.

I kicked her icy feet aside, pulled the coverlet down and said sternly, "Bid, stop behaving like a simpleton. Is it a ghost you are scared of?"

"Yes!" she squeaked, and tried to cover her face again, but I wouldn't let her. "I swear I never slept a wink last night, with all the creaks and squeaks and sobbing moans."

"The creaks and squeaks were almost certainly Jack moving around in a strange place, or my bed creaking, and the sobbing moans…" I stopped. I know I cried last night, though I did try to be quiet.

"Who is this keeper?" I asked, getting up to shut the door firmly and pick up Jack. I do not believe there are such things as ghosts – after all, I have never seen one, but I take no chances. "Why is he called the keeper?"

She looked at me as if it were I who'd lost her wits. "Because he keeps things. Kept things. Oh, Mistress Makepeace, before they cleared this place out for you and your brother—" She stopped. "Where is your brother?"

"Never mind him," I said. "You were saying about before they cleared this place out…"

"It were full!"

"Full of what?"

"Full of things he kept. He used to walk the lanes for hours, and his eyes were always on the ground and he would pick up anything he found and keep it. That's why he was the keeper. Oh, there were such things here. Still are, some of them. I saw them while I was getting the place ready."

I was losing patience with the silly girl. "What things?"

"Well, a badger's skull, and a closet full of old rags as you wouldn't make a floor cloth out of, and sticks and funny-shaped stones, and mountains and mountains of fir cones, and old bones, and a whole cheese that must have been twenty years old it stunk so rotten, and a coffin with no one in it—"

"A what?"

"A coffin with no one in it, and shrivelled cider apples, and drawings he did that were weirder than anything I've ever seen, and bits of broken guns that weren't no good, and a wasp's nest with no wasps, and four complete birds' wings and I can't remember no more, Mistress."

"That's quite enough, Bid, but tell me, why do you think he's a ghost?"

"He's dead, and he's been seen, Mistress, and them as do see him – they dies."

I thought about that. "How do you know?"

She patted Jack (for which I liked her) and snuggled down. "Because that's what happens."

I lay down too. "But if they die when they see him, how do you know they've seen him? They cannot tell you if they're dead."

Bid smiled sleepily. "'Tis true, Mistress."

And now it is morning, and I have walked outside. Though it is cold, the air is crisp and clear and Jack and I both have wet feet from the dewy grass. Beautiful.

Later

Bid busied herself this morning, trying to clean out my clothes chest. It has a stale, musty smell which seems to creep around the whole room. I took time to look around my new home. It is a little rough and ready, but it has been prettily furnished, on the whole, and I'm sure I will soon be cosy. I have not examined the outbuildings yet. I know that Bid has thrown much of the keeper's collection into one of them.

Just a short way away are the gates to Gracy Park. I shall be able to see everyone coming and going! And if I wish to leave the park, why, nothing could be quicker or easier. Though why I should wish to leave, I cannot imagine. There are walks aplenty here, that's for sure, though there is nothing else to do. I must grow flowers! Lots of flowers! And vegetables, too.

I ate my midday dinner alone, as Bid wanted to go to the dairy for milk (and a little gossip with the dairymaids, no doubt). I daydreamed about Dominic. How was he faring? Had he reached the port safely? How long will he have to wait for a ship? How wonderful life will be when he returns!

Jack, out in our little garden, gave a sudden bark, which snapped me from my daydream. I looked around and suddenly saw my life as it really is. Without warning, I was in floods of tears. Tears for my poor, dead mother, tears for my brother, who I may not see for years, but mostly tears for myself. It suddenly hit me that I am alone. There is no one to love me.

Except my Jack! I hurried out to him, to see why he'd barked, and found him rolling on the ground with Godfrey.

"Good day!" I cried, wiping away my tears.

They both ran to me.

"Good day, cousin," said Godfrey. "Your eyes are fat and red, did you know?" Then he clapped a hand to his mouth. "Sorry. Mama says I mustn't be honest with ladies."

I laughed. "It doesn't matter. A visit from you is just what I need to cheer me up!"

"I really came to visit Jack," he said. Honest again!

"Then we are both glad of your company," I said. And I was.

While Godfrey and Jack raced around together, I wondered where Bid had got to. Then I began wondering what to do with her and her silly fears. I have always been brought up to believe what I see, not to see what I believe. At least, that's how my mother explained it. She said I wasn't to assume something was real simply because I had imagined it, and she went to great lengths to explain that the tales she told me by firelight were not true. She had made them up, especially for me.

I had to find out about this stupid ghost story.

Godfrey took me and Jack for a long walk around Gracy Park. It is enormous, and quite beautiful even before spring has really got going. There are two lakes, each with many water birds, and a deer park, and a wide stream which feeds the lakes, cutting almost through the middle of the whole estate. Godfrey showed me the cottages where some of the Gracy Park tenants live. They are poor people, that's clear. But, I reflected, I wager none is as poor as me, for I am totally dependent on the goodwill of the de Gracy family. Oh, how I wish they were all as charming as Godfrey.

"I would like a dog," he said, throwing a short fat twig for Jack to fetch.

"I think you would probably like one cleverer than him!" I said. My dog picked up the stick and, instead of retrieving it and bringing it back to Godfrey, he ran off with it. "Jack expects you to run after him."

"Then I will!"

And the two of them had the most glorious romp, which only ended when Jack got too close to the lake and some angry ducks flew at him, quacking crossly.

"Godfrey," I asked, "what can you tell me about Keeper's Cottage?"

"Not much," he said. "I've never been inside. Everyone is frightened they'll see the keeper's ghost."

"Do you believe in ghosts?"

"Of course. Don't you?"

"Oh yes," I said, wishing to please him.

"Then why do you stay there?"

How could I tell him I would rather face something unseen than be swallowed up in the de Gracy household? I am Susannah Makepeace, who will one day be carried away by her knight in shining armour – her brother. I must be free to go. If I lived with the de Gracys, I would become someone's companion, someone's waiting woman. Someone would come to rely on me – I might even come to care for someone. No. I must remain free. I just wish I was independent.

February 15th

I spend my days walking with Jack, chatting with Bid, and helping her to make Keeper's Cottage a pleasant place to live in. She still has her night terrors, bless her, and sometimes her fear is infectious. But I have seen nothing ghostly yet, so I do my best to keep the nights calm. Soon she will be brave enough to sleep in her own room, I'm sure.

I have had little contact with the de Gracy family. Food is sent to me, or else Bid fetches it. I sometimes see Juliana when I'm out walking, but she will not come close when Jack is with me. Lady Anne has called twice to see how I'm faring. She doesn't stay long in the cottage – obviously she fears what people believe is here. I don't mind that she doesn't stay. It's not easy talking to someone who is on edge all the time.

Life is not exciting, but perhaps it is better so.

March 1st

A letter from Dominic. How my heart leapt when I saw his writing! But then my heart sank. He has still not left England! I had hoped he was well on his way, perhaps a few hundred miles nearer his goal, and almost a month nearer our reunion.

He expects that he and Ned will take ship within a day or two. He is fast running out of money, and must go soon.

March 3rd

I worry so much about Dominic that I find I cannot concentrate on a thing. This morning Bid asked me if I knew where the blue butter dish was, and I said I would get it. I went upstairs and brought down my chamber pot! And then, after I had broken my fast with some of yesterday's bread, I put the dried-up bits of crust in my sewing box instead of outside for the birds.

At least the weather is warmer. Bid and I left the kitchen door open nearly all day, and the cottage smells less of wood smoke now.

March 8th

I thought my life in Devon was dull, but at least I had the odd moment of excitement, like milking the cow, or washing my stockings. Here there is nothing – absolutely nothing – to do, because Bid does everything. I have explored the house. I have explored the outbuildings. One is now stacked almost to the rafters with the keeper's keepings. I was taken aback to see the barrel of a gun pointing at me from beneath a heap of old rags, but Bid pulled it out and showed me that was all it was – just the barrel.

"There be bits of guns all over the place, Mistress Susannah," she said. "They won't harm you none, not in bits."

"They would if someone put the bits together," I retorted.

She laughed. "Who would do that? Me?"

"No," I said, advancing slowly upon her. "The keeper!"

How she screamed!

To be truthful, I do have moments of excitement, but they are all at night, when Bid's nerves and imagination get the better of her, and she is convinced the ghost of the keeper is coming up the stairs. I know, of course, that should anyone – or anything – make its way into the house, my Jack would bark. But it is delicious fun to pretend to be scared! Bid still refuses to sleep alone, which is annoying. No, if I'm honest, I don't mind having her company, apart from her occasional snorts. She sleeps on a mattress on the floor beside me, and will not be alone in any room at night if she can help it. Even during the day, when I'm out walking, she leaves the house-cleaning or the cooking and works on the little vegetable garden, which she's attempting to clear.

Bid insists on doing all the work. She says it is her place, and that it is my place to be a lady. Little does she know that in my heart I am no lady. I am not (as my mother used to tease me) a rumpscuttle, but I have always been ready to ride a horse, run with Jack, climb a tree, paddle in a stream.

However, as I am always aware that Lady Anne or the awful Juliana might visit, I do not do these things. I sew or read the Bible, which is my only book. Once I sang for a while, but only once, because Bid gave me such tight-lipped looks that I thought it best to stop.

Oh, I am so frustrated! If Bid did not sleep here, I would go out into the moonlight and dance under the stars and sing to the owls. Anything not to be cooped up like a pet canary.

The one good bit of news is that there is no news from Dominic. It must mean he has taken ship at last. It must!

March 14th

Juliana is a – a – a mullipuff! I cannot think of anything nice to say about her.

She called today and checked my pantry.

"Yes, Susan, you have enough food for a couple of days. Mama will arrange for Bid to fetch more shortly."

Then she checked that the cottage was clean. She pretended she was just looking round, but I saw her run her hand along a shelf and then she examined her glove, which was spotless. One of the cushions in the parlour gave out a small cloud of dust when she banged it. (I suspect that Juliana would give out a cloud of dust if I banged *her*.)

"Susan, you must learn to control your servants. Keep checking Bid's work."

Then she caught sight of a deep bowl of wild daffodils I had picked among the trees near the stream. "Who arranged those?"

Bid bobbed a curtsey. "I did, m'lady."

Juliana tutted, then she pulled and poked and stuffed and

prodded until she'd arranged the flowers to her satisfaction. They stood up, each separate and ignoring the others. She stepped back, head on one side, and said, "There, Susan – much better, I think, don't you?"

"Very natural-looking," I said. This was obviously the wrong thing to say because she gave me a slit-eyed look, her lips pinched so tight I could scarcely see them.

The daffodils actually looked a lot better the way Bid did them – as if they were growing in a garden and the breeze was upon them.

"Flowers are best arranged by the lady of the house, you know, Susan," said Juliana.

When she had finished her tour of inspection, which I'm sure was kindly meant, I offered her refreshment.

"Thank you, Susan, no."

I had the feeling she wouldn't lower herself to drinking out of the cups in Keeper's Cottage.

I walked with her to the garden gate then asked something which had been niggling me.

"Cousin Juliana, why do you call me Susan? It is not my name."

She looked down at me, smiling her narrow smile, but said nothing.

"Cousin Juliana, my given name is Susannah. It may be different here, but where I come from, Susan is more likely to be thought of as a servant's name."

She smiled again, her thin lips stretched more widely this time.

"I think Susan suits you very well, cousin."

I pressed my lips together, trying not to speak hastily. But it is a fault of mine – I often do.

"I do not like you calling me Susan, cousin Juliana. You make me feel as if I am just a – a – a poor relation."

She looked at me, slightly puzzled. "Well, you are, aren't you?"

I took a deep breath. For once I held my tongue and strode indoors. "Bid!" I said. "It's about to rain. Fetch in the washing."

She looked out. "It b'ain't gonna rain, Mistress!"

I turned on her, and I know my face must have been full of fury. "Go!"

She scuttled outside, muttering to herself.

I went to the shelf and picked up the Makepeace family Bible. Clasping it between my hands, I made a solemn vow that, while I would accept the de Gracy family's charity because it is well meant (and I have no choice), I will never, ever ask them for anything. Not for anything at all!

March 17th

I am still fuming over Juliana's insensitive tongue. Doesn't she realize how hateful it is for me to be here, dependent on people whom, until a few weeks ago, I had scarcely heard of?

Oh, I loathe this place! Everything conspires to drive me mad, even Bid, with her constant chatter and her never-ending twittering about the keeper's ghost. Well, I'd like to meet that ghost right now – the mood I am in, he would do well to avoid me, for I would most certainly punch him on the nose.

Even now, when she's in the garden and knows I'm busy writing, she twitters on about a man on the hill yonder, on a horse. Does she really think the keeper's ghost could ride a horse? I shall close the window.

Bid is right. It is a man on a horse. And the horse looks familiar, even from this distance.

Later

Oh, how my heart leapt when I realized that I did know that horse. It was Moonbeam, so named for the streak of white which runs diagonally down across his face, like moonlight seen through trees. Dominic's horse!

I must have flown down the stairs, for suddenly I was outside, running up the hill, shouting and waving to my brother, not even realizing I was barefoot!

The rider dismounted and stood silhouetted against the sky. And I faltered, then stopped. He was not Dominic. He was not tall enough. Not only that, but one shoulder drooped. One leg was bent, while the other was straight.

It was Ned. As soon as I realized this, it felt as if my heart had plunged into my stomach. Ned here, on Dominic's horse. Oh, the things that went through my mind in the seconds that I stared at him. Over all of them, the one that hammered at my brain was the realization that Dominic must be dead. Why else would Ned be here with my brother's horse? Unless, unless he had harmed Dominic in some way?

I flew at him. "Ned! Ned Allin! Tell me, tell me the truth,

do not spare me! What of my brother? Is he hurt? Or worse? Oh, say not worse!"

Ned shook his head and smiled gently. "Nay, Mistress Susannah, Master Dominic is in good health. Well, in fairly good health. Truth to tell, he did have a slight fever when I saw him last, but he is aboard ship for America. Long gone now. He sends his dearest love, and is sorry he could not write a final letter, but it all happened so quickly in the end. Getting on the ship and such."

I took Ned back down to the cottage, and sent Bid for some beer and cheese and bread for him. When she returned, I told her she could go and see her mother and brothers and sisters for the rest of the day. Ned was my old friend, I explained, and I wished to spend time with him, to catch up on all the news.

She wished us a pleasant visit, curtsied and went to go, but I called her back.

"Bid, I do not wish anyone to know that my friend is here. Please remember that." I wasn't sure if I could trust her, so I added (nastily, I know), "If you do not remember, you will have to sleep in your own room."

She actually looked hurt, which made me feel rather mean. "You can always trust me, Mistress."

When she'd gone, Ned told me all. He and Dominic had waited so long for a ship that they'd been forced to use a large part of my brother's money, just to live.

"We had to sell my old mare," said Ned, "for money for food and lodging. We didn't get much for her, love her heart."

"But why are *you* not aboard?" I asked. "And Moonbeam, too?"

"Money, Mistress Susannah," he said. "We didn't have enough to pay my passage, and the captain refused to take Moonbeam. He said he was doing Master Dominic a favour by giving him a place when he was full to the gunnels already. If he wanted to go, the horse stayed. If he wanted the horse to go, he could wait for another ship."

"And he would not wait?"

"No, Mistress." Ned took a huge swig of ale, and I refilled his cup. "Master Dominic said the sooner he got to America, the sooner he would make his fortune and return for you." He hesitated. "And for me."

"He said that?"

"Yes, Mistress. He said that if I came back and watched over you, he would see that all would be well for me on his return. I will never want for work. That's what he said."

My dear brother.

March 19th

I expect Ned will call today. He left the day before yesterday to find somewhere he can work in exchange for lodgings. I hope he finds someone kind, who will not mind that he is not quick to move.

March 20th

It is almost midday. Ned has not come yet. He will come soon, I am sure.

How I wish I had a book to read. I know I have our Bible, but in truth, I would love some poems or a tale to lose myself in. Time passes slowly. Bid says that Juliana has books.

"What sort?" I asked, unthinking.

"How should I know, Mistress Susannah? I could not read the names even if I dared touch them."

"They are sure to be dry and dusty and full of passages

about improving oneself," I said bitterly. I regretted it instantly, because Bid understood and giggled.

If she were not a servant, Bid and I might be friends. I have no one else, except Ned, and even he has not bothered to visit me.

March 22nd

Ned came! And he's caught three fat trout for us! It's been a beautiful spring day, warm and sunny, and Bid called me from my seat against our one old apple tree, saying, "Your young man is here again, Mistress."

Does she disapprove? Well, if she does, what is that to me?

Ned has found both work and lodging at an inn called the Stag's Head in the bottom of a valley. It's beside a swift-flowing river that has a trout stream running gently alongside it, with a raised footpath between the two. He says the countryside reminds him of the deep hills around Lustleigh. I should like to see it.

I offered to show him Gracy Park, so he tied Moonbeam to the door of my little barn, and we walked as he told me about his new home.

"My work is just feeding the fires," he said, "and chopping wood and collecting the pots, and helping with horses and so on. But 'tis honest work." He frowned slightly. "At least, I think it is."

I thought that an odd remark, but he said no more.

"And Moonbeam?" I asked. "Can you stable him there?"

"By rights, he is yours, Mistress Susannah. And it would not be wise for me to keep him at the Stag's Head. The landlord said Moonbeam's a fine animal, and many would be glad to own him. 'Better keep your eye on that horse, lad,' he said, and I think he meant it well. Oh, and he has a good wife, called Kate. She said their son was lame, too – much worse than me – and they are glad to offer me work."

"See?" I said. "You have been here just a few days and you have acquaintances already. I still have none."

We reached the lake, so I sat on a log, for I could see Ned's leg was aching. He settled on the grass beside me and I explained about the de Gracy family, and made him smile when I imitated the ghastly Juliana!

I was strutting about, tossing supercilious remarks over my shoulder, when Ned leapt to his feet and pulled off his hat. I spun round. There behind me were two fine chestnut horses bearing none other than Juliana and her father.

"Whatever are you doing, Susan?" asked Juliana.

"I, um, I was reciting a poem." I was so taken aback that I forgot to correct her misuse of my name.

"'Tis like no poem I know," she went on spitefully. "May Papa and I hear it, too?"

Thankfully, Sir Roger wasn't the sort of man to have the patience for poetry. He raised his whip and pointed it at Ned.

"Who are you?"

I noticed he did not address Ned as "sir". But it wasn't surprising. My poor friend is ill-dressed, and not well-groomed.

"Forgive me," I said. "Sir Roger, cousin Juliana, may I present Ned Allin, my, er, my…"

"I used to work for the Makepeace family, Sir Roger," said Ned. "I am here to return Master Dominic's horse to Mistress Susannah."

Juliana's mount was insolent enough to attempt to munch a mouthful of grass without permission. She yanked its head up. "So, Susan, you wish your horse to join ours, do you? Is there room in our stables, I wonder?"

"There is no need," I said. "Ned will stable Moonbeam at the Stag's Head, where he now works."

Sir Roger almost exploded. "He will not!" he barked. "Luke can fit out one of the outbuildings of Keeper's Cottage as a stable." He swung his horse's head round. "The Stag's Head indeed!"

Juliana cantered away, but Sir Roger spoke over his shoulder to Ned. "Stay off my land. I'll have no one from the Stag's Head in Gracy Park."

And with that he was gone.

I am furious. Not only have they done exactly as they wish without consulting my feelings, but they have put me even deeper in their debt. Moonbeam is to be the latest recipient of their charity. For how can I feed a horse and clean a stable? I am a girl. Where would I find hay and straw? I shall be dependent on one of Luke's stable lads.

Just to spite Sir Roger, I took Ned home with me and we all ate the trout.

March 26th

Bid has been gossiping in the kitchen of the big house, that's clear. She knows Ned has been banished from Gracy Park. I was picking burrs from Jack's coat, when she came outside to weed the bean patch.

"How will you see your friend now, Mistress Susannah?"

I didn't reply. For see Ned I will, somehow.

After a while, I asked, "Where is the Stag's Head, Bid?"

She drew a sharp breath. "Ooh, you don't want to be going near there, Mistress. Things go on there."

"But I'm told the landlord is a good man," I said.

"Sykes MacPhee? Oh, he's lived round these parts ever

since his father settled here. Yes, he's a good man, always tries to please everybody. That's his trouble, being pleasing. No one has anything bad to say about Sykes MacPhee. Or his wife. Kate MacPhee is kind."

I tugged impatiently at a small prickly twig that obstinately refused to be pulled out of Jack's fur. "What do you mean, 'That's his trouble?' And what is wrong with the Stag's Head?"

She looked around as if she was afraid someone might hear. "They do say that Sykes MacPhee turns a blind eye to goings-on."

"Goings-on?"

"Men who drink at the Stag's Head are not all as honest and straightforward as Sykes MacPhee. They gather there and share their spoils—"

"Spoils?" This was a whole new language to me.

"Things they've stolen. Robbers meet at the Stag's Head. Highwaymen, too, I wouldn't be surprised," said Bid.

"You cannot know that for sure," I said, "and anyway, if this Sykes MacPhee is such a good, upright, honest citizen," (I did try not to sound sarcastic), "then why does he allow goings-on?"

Bid swore at a thistle stump that refused to leave the ground.

"Well? Why does he?"

"I don't know, Mistress. Maybe he's scared not to. Maybe

it's more than his life's worth to cross certain people. Like as not, he wouldn't have any customers in his inn if he put a stop to goings-on."

I do hope Ned will be all right. I thought back to Bid's original question. How shall I manage to see him? He's banned from Gracy Park, and the Stag's Head is certainly not for me.

March 29th

Moonbeam's stable is ready and I've made a decision. I will not accept any more of the de Gracy bounty than I have to. I must eat and I must have shelter and I must sleep. My horse must eat and have shelter. Therefore I am happy to accept the charity of a house, a bed and food, and Moonbeam is happy to accept food and shelter. But more than that I will not. I shall look after Moonbeam myself. He'll be my responsibility, and when Dominic returns, his horse will shine with good health. Moonbeam will, of course, learn to love me, so it may be difficult for Dominic to regain his affection!

I explained my feelings to Luke. We had a very polite little argument about it, which I won. He will send down everything Moonbeam needs in the way of food and bedding. Feed. They call it feed, not food, when it's for a horse. We are agreed that if I have any problems with the saddle or anything, I am to tell him.

"We won't bother the family with little things like that, eh, Mistress?" he said, and he gave me one of his wicked winks.

I do believe I have a friend there.

April 4th

Juliana and her waiting woman met me walking through the long avenue of limes today. I was watching squirrels and thinking how the darker red parts of their fur are much like the colour of Dominic's hair.

"Good day, Susan," she said. "Why, you look quite far away! Do tell me your thoughts. Is your mind in America, with your brother? Or perhaps it is with another? Maybe your brother will return – if he returns – to find you a married woman." She laughed. Then she saw my face.

"I only tease you, Susan. But you will have to think about your future, will you not?"

I knew what she meant. Marriage. Even the waiting woman knew what she meant and stepped aside, pretending to examine a large yellow toadstool.

"Cousin Juliana," I said, "I regret – as much as you obviously do – having to throw myself on your family's charity. Your parents are very good to me, and when Dominic returns—"

She smirked. I swear she did.

"When Dominic returns, he will take the burden from your family. And," I said, getting carried away, "I am quite sure he will repay the kindness of Sir Roger and Lady Anne, many times over. In the meantime, I have plans of my own to repay them, I promise you that. Good day to you both."

And off I went, leaving Juliana and her waiting woman open-mouthed.

At least, I hope I left them open-mouthed. I didn't have the courage to look round to see.

Plans? I have no plans.

April 6th

I picked bluebells this morning after church. They are early here, perhaps because Gracy Park is so sheltered. The flowers, even in April, are abundant, and I only ever pick the wild ones. The weather is gentle and calm. I've always loved the spring, and here it is beautiful indeed, with birds and buds everywhere. I should be happy if only I had someone of my own.

I feel mean to write that. I have my Jack, bless him.

Wait! I do have someone else of my own!

Later

I shocked Bid this afternoon. I put on my hooded cloak as if I was going for a stroll around Gracy Park, and the next time she saw me was when I called her from outside our gate.

"Bid! Look at me!"

She came to the door drying her hands on her apron, and stared, speechless. Then she ran to me, saying, "Do be careful, Mistress. That's a big 'un, that Moonbeam is!"

I looked down at her and laughed. "Don't worry, Bid. I can manage him. Why don't you fetch him one of those old carrots you're using for pottage? Then he'll be your friend for life."

She hurried off, glancing nervously over her shoulder, and returned with a woody, pale carrot.

"Hold your hand out flat."

She did so.

I sighed. "Bid, hold your hand out flat with the carrot *on* it."

She laughed nervously. "You don't mean for that great brute to bite it off my hand, do you, Mistress? Not me!" She flung the carrot to the ground, and Moonbeam picked it up and began crunching. When he'd eaten it, he whinnied and showed his teeth, as he always does after a treat. Bid squealed and jumped back! Luckily, Moonbeam isn't nervous!

"See?" I said, as the horse dipped his head and nuzzled Jack's nose. "Even little Jack isn't afraid of Moonbeam." And I bunched up my skirts in front of me, waved goodbye and set off. I'd like to have put on Dominic's old breeches once more, but the thought of Juliana's disgust and scorn prevented me. I still have them, though. When I've ridden Moonbeam all around Gracy Park, and I know the ground well, I shall don breeches, hat and cloak and ride in moonlight. Ha! Maybe I'll be seen and become known as the Night Rider! That'll take everyone's mind off the keeper!

April 11th

My days are long, even though we go to bed early. Today seemed extra long. Bid spent most of the day making bread and pastry and salting some left-over meat, to stop it going bad. I tried to help, but she said – very politely – that she prefers to get on with the cooking herself. I know what she means. I am not helpful, as I tend to either daydream or talk too much. I took my Bible out and sat under the apple tree. I have read much of it, of course, but now that it is my only book, I have started it from the beginning and intend to read it all the way through, every word.

I soon wearied of reading how this person begat that one, and that one begat this one, and laid the book aside. As I did so, I noticed Bid gazing at me out of a window. She is, I believe, a good girl, and I think she likes me. She never says anything against the de Gracy family, though I have yet to hear her say anything nice about them.

Last night I lay awake until almost dawn – the birds had started singing, which was a welcome change from Bid's night-time snorts. I couldn't sleep because I couldn't stop wondering. Wondering how Dominic is faring on the ocean. Wondering what is happening with Ned. Wondering how I can fulfil my promise to Juliana. The thing is, I can't. How can I possibly repay my benefactors? I have nothing. I own only my clothes, my Bible, my writing things and Moonbeam. The first three I could not survive without, and the last is not really mine to give.

However, if I have no ideas, maybe Lady Anne has.

Later

I rode Moonbeam early this morning, with Jack running along beside us, then walked to the big house after Bid and I had eaten our dinner. I have asked her to share my table. It is silly that I should eat in one room and she in the kitchen. I would like to make a friend of Bid, but is she trustworthy? Heaven knows, I've always found it hard to keep a still tongue in my own head. Why should I expect a simple, uneducated girl to do so?

I stopped at the stables to give Jack to Luke, who offered to find him a bone, then made my way to the house. Lady Anne received me graciously and called for some tea, which was generous of her, as it is so expensive. However, I'm sure cost never enters the de Gracy heads, though it does surprise me that much of the furniture and hangings are slightly – well, shabby. Perhaps Sir Roger is mean, for they must have money enough, living in such a grand house. Mustn't they?

I came straight to the point. "I am unused to living by the kindness of others, Lady Anne," I said, "and I find it very difficult. We Makepeaces have independent spirits."

She tried to interrupt, but I continued. "I wish to offer my services in some way, in order to help repay you for my board and lodgings."

"Dear cousin Susannah," she said, "that is unnecessary. We are all glad to be of service to you in your time of need. Your mother was my kinswoman, and I like to think that if dear Juliana had been in need, she would have been offered the same hospitality."

The idea of Juliana with my mother made a giggle rise into my throat, but without warning, it turned into a sob.

"My dear, you are overwrought," said Lady Anne. "Let us have no more talk of performing services – ah, here is the tea. And Godfrey! Come and join us, sweeting."

I smiled at Godfrey, who greeted me warmly. He sat at a small table and emptied his pockets on to it. Acorns, pebbles, a cone, a large seed-head. He's as bad as the keeper!

As the maid laid out the cups, I began again, "Lady Anne, if only I could—"

But she put a finger to her lips. "*Pas devant la bonne.*"

I wasn't surprised she didn't want me to speak in front of the maid. It wouldn't do to have a member of the de Gracy family – however distant – talking about performing menial services.

When the tea was poured, I lifted my cup and sipped. It was vile. Strong and dark. My mother and I rarely drank tea, but when we did it was always golden and fragrant.

"Mama," said Godfrey, "I wish you would teach me French. You're always speaking it, and I don't understand."

She smiled. "My pet, my French may impress you, but it is not good at all. You shall have a French tutor one day, of course you shall."

"Me!" I blurted.

They stared.

"Me!" I said again. "I could teach Godfrey French. I speak it well. I was taught by my mother. Oh, please, Lady Anne, let me do this. It would be one way I could be of service." I stopped and looked at Godfrey. "If you wish it, too."

He grinned. "Only if you teach me at Keeper's Cottage!"

Lady Anne looked appalled. "Not there, Godfrey."

"I don't mind it in the daytime, Mama," he said, "and I can play with Jack afterwards."

And so it was agreed. I left in higher spirits than I've been in for a while.

I also realized that Lady Anne let me go to live in Keeper's Cottage, when she knew about the so-called ghost. Oh, well, I suppose I did insist.

April 14th

Godfrey and I had our first French lesson today. The first word I taught him was, of course, *chien*! He immediately ran out into the garden calling, "*Chien! Chien!*" Jack would have followed Godfrey even if he'd called him "*Chat*"! That seemed to be the end of our lesson, so I went out to play, too. But I will take my duty more seriously next time.

He took me back with him, because Lady Anne wanted to ask me how his lesson went. I quickly taught him to say *Bonjour, Maman* and *merci*, so he could at least greet her and thank her for something.

Lady Anne commented on my peaky looks, which was hardly tactful of her, I must say. I can see where Godfrey gets his honesty from. But with him it's charming, from Lady Anne it's insulting.

She blamed my recent upheavals and said I probably hadn't been eating properly lately.

"I will see that Bid brings you extra good things from the kitchen," she said.

More charity. More pity! Just what I do not want.

April 18th

I caught my boot heel in my skirt today as I dismounted from Moonbeam, and tore a jagged rent in the material. Oh, men do not realize how lucky they are to be able to move freely.

I decided Moonbeam could wait for me to sort him out, so I just took off his saddle and bridle. Then I sat mending the skirt without taking it off, and when Bid brought in some knot biscuits, still warm from the oven, she looked at my stitching and tutted, and said she would finish it for me. Well, what she actually said was, "For heaven's sake, Mistress, keep your hands out of that sewing basket or we'll all be going round looking like something the keeper's dragged back in. Oooh!" she added, and ran to touch wood as she realized who – or what – she'd been talking about. We have had better nights lately, and I was annoyed that she'd reminded herself of her ghost!

I felt fidgety as she sewed, and was about to undo my skirt and step out of it so I could be free, when I heard footsteps on the path, and Godfrey poked his head through the window. "*Bonjour, Mademoiselle Susannah!*"

"*Bonjour, mon cousin,*" I replied. "*Entrez!*"

He looked puzzled at that instruction, which I have not yet taught him. I repeated it and beckoned, so he would understand. Now I was glad to be still inside my skirt.

"Jack didn't warn us of Master Godfrey coming," Bid pointed out. "They must be firm friends now."

Godfrey was pleased at that. We sat for our lesson until my skirt was mended.

"Thank you, Bid," I said. "That's perfect. You may go now."

She curtsied. "*Merci*, Mistress." And with a cheeky smile, she was gone.

Bid is not so dim after all. Perhaps I could teach her to read. What a kindness that would be. And it would fill my hours. I must think about it. I would like to be known as a kind mistress. I cannot be a generous one, as I have nothing to give. But I could give my time.

April 24th

I feel the need to see Ned. It has been a long time. I would like to know that he is all right. Whenever I ride out on Moonbeam I look for him, but he has not appeared. I cannot blame him. Sir Roger was most threatening.

I just hope nothing has happened to him at the Stag's Head. Surely no one would hurt a poor lame boy?

April 27th

I am concerned about Ned. I asked Bid if she had ever been to the Stag's Head.

"No, but I seen it, o' course," was the reply.

"Is it far?"

"Oh, 'tis a good way."

"Could you walk there?" I asked casually.

She looked at me as if I were not quite sane. "Mistress, you can walk anywhere. Just some places takes longer than others, see?"

I did not speak hastily. I would like to have boxed Bid's ears for impertinence, but I wanted information. "And is the distance to the Stag's Head one of the longer ones?"

"Depends," she said.

I just looked at her. "Well," she said defensively, "if you think it's a long way to the front gate, then it's a very long way to the Stag's Head. But if you think it's not all that far to – well, to some place I never been to – then it's not far to the Stag's Head. See?"

I laughed. I did see.

"Could I ride there, Bid? Oh, not that I want to," I said, seeing the expression on her face. "It would just give me an idea of … of how far…"

"*Someone* could ride there," she said, "but not you, Mistress. You'm not wanting to see that Ned friend of yours, are you?"

"No," I lied, and my eyes filled with tears. I blinked them away, but the more I blinked, the wetter my face became.

"You do!" said Bid. "Well, why didn't you say so? I can get a message to him, no trouble. Oh, here's Jack, wanting something to eat. Come on, my handsome."

Off she went with my beloved dog. I could have kissed her.

May 2nd

I was bundling herbs in the kitchen this afternoon, when Bid, who'd been gazing out of the window on and off, suddenly grabbed my hand and pulled me towards her.

"Look, Mistress," she said.

"What?" There were raindrops from the last shower, still dripping off the roof, but that was all.

"There! In the trees yonder. Down by the gates."

At first I could see nothing, then I noticed a flash of something light. A hand, waving!

"Ned!" I cried.

Indeed it was, and he was soon at the kitchen table, enjoying a big steaming bowl of Bid's good pottage.

"Right tasty this is, Mistress," he said.

I smiled. "You have Bid to thank for that."

He looked up at her. "Thank you, Bid. Is that really your name?"

"Sort of," she said. "It's short for Biddy, which is short for Bridget, which is my long name. I couldn't say it when I was little, and I used to say Bid. No one calls me Bridget. They all call me Bid."

"And my name is Edward," said Ned. "But no one calls me that any more."

"Then we're two of a kind," said Bid.

I decided to stop this private conversation. "Bid," I said, "Ned is my good friend, and I am glad to see him. I thank you for sending a message to the Stag's Head—"

"Right surprised I was to get it, Mistress Susannah, and I came as soon as I could!"

"Yes, I'm sure, but let me finish, Ned. Bid, please don't tell anyone at the house that Ned has been here. I think Sir Roger would be quite unforgiving, and that would make life even lonelier for me."

Bid looked as if she'd been struck dumb. I began to think

I'd made a dreadful mistake in trusting her. But then she spoke, through tight lips.

"Mistress Makepeace, I am your servant. You are the only person in Gracy Park what treats me like a yooman being. I would never tell your secrets."

She paused for a moment, then whirled round and stamped up the stairs. Ned and I looked at each other.

"Oh dear," I said, "I have hurt her feelings."

Footsteps stamped down the stairs. Bid stalked into the room and handed me a book. It was bound in softest brown leather, and when I opened the cover, I saw written inside, "Juliana de Gracy".

I looked into my maid's defiant eyes. "Bid, did you..."

"Did I what, Mistress? Did I steal it? No! I borrowed it. I borrowed it for *you*. 'Cos I know you likes to read, and I seen you get fed up with that there Bible. I borrowed it for you to read something different. I was going to take it to you next time you went to sit under the apple tree, as a surprise." She folded her arms. "Now, would I a done that if I was going to tell your secrets?"

What could I do? I threw my arms round her and hugged her. I am not *so* alone.

May 25th

With Bid's help, Ned has visited often. He likes his work at the Stag's Head, and he says Sykes MacPhee and his wife have been truly kind to him. They warn him to be careful of certain customers, and when to stay clear of a group of men huddled together and whispering.

"What do they whisper about?" I asked.

"I dunno, Mistress, but there's one man who comes in regular. He takes the things they've stolen and gives them money. Then he fences the stuff – that means he sells it. Lots of the customers look out for him. He even gets free ale. He just calls for a tankard and then glares at Sykes MacPhee until he goes away."

I wish Ned didn't have to work there, but he says no one even notices him, so I mustn't worry.

June 2nd

I am very suspicious. Juliana is being *nice* to me. Oh, she still looks down her nose, but she is definitely trying to be pleasant. In church yesterday, she kept catching my eye, and nodding. Most peculiar.

I wonder why.

June 7th

I so enjoy my rides out on Moonbeam. Today I was walking him carefully down the steep hillside into the long narrow valley that borders Gracy Park on the west, when I spied Ned walking along the opposite bank of the fast-flowing river.

"*Ned!*" I called.

He looked up, and I swear he saw me. For a moment I thought he was about to wave. But no, he completely ignored me.

"Ned!"

He strode on in his bobbing, dipping fashion.

At first I was livid that he was deliberately ignoring me, for I was sure he was. And then I felt hurt.

I swung Moonbeam's head round and headed back uphill. As I did so, I gasped in fear. Although I was facing the sun, I could see, silhouetted against the skyline, a figure on horseback.

I thought my heart might stop. Should I flee? I had nothing a highwayman would want – just my clothes and my cloak. But then…

"Sweet Susan!" the figure cried, and the horse moved towards me.

Now the sun was no longer behind her, I could see Juliana's thin-lipped face quite clearly. I attempted to smile, but my mouth was so dry that my lips stuck to my teeth.

"Juliana," I croaked, eventually.

"Why, you look as if you have seen a ghost," she said. "The keeper isn't worrying you, is he?"

A lot you'd care if he was, I thought.

We trotted along, side by side. Juliana glanced at my bunched-up skirts. "Why do you not ride side-saddle?" she asked. "It is so ungainly, to ride astride, like a man."

So I'm ungainly, am I?

"I have a spare side-saddle that I shall send to you," she said, firmly. "My father would not care to see you ride in this manner, Susan."

Nice as she's being, she still cannot bring herself to call me Susannah.

"I thank you, cousin," I said, "but I manage very well with my own saddle." In truth, Luke offered to lend me a side-saddle, but I chose not to accept. And I did not mention his kindness, for fear of getting him into trouble.

Juliana was determined to have her own way. "Nonsense," she said. "Come now, you mustn't be too proud to take help. After all, you are not in a position to be so, are you?"

Witch.

Later

It is only now that I've realized why Ned ignored me. Of course! He'd already seen Juliana, and did not wish me to get into trouble with Sir Roger. For if I had been caught actually talking to Ned, there's no doubt that Juliana would have gone straight to her father.

June 9th

The side-saddle has arrived, and Luke took the trouble to show me how to fit it. When I was small I watched our groom do it often enough, and it is not so different from an ordinary saddle, for goodness' sake. I have had to learn how to do that.

I hate the side saddle already. I do not want anything associated with Juliana near my Moonbeam. I shall not use it.

June 13th

Of course I do use the side-saddle. At least, I use it whenever I think I'm likely to meet anyone in Gracy Park. But in the evenings, when the light is beginning to go, and I know they are all indoors, I put the old saddle on Moonbeam and go for a gallop. I do not feel safe even cantering when riding side-saddle. Because you sit that little bit higher, it makes a lot of difference when riding beneath trees. I don't want a branch to knock my head off!

However, when I ride astride, I can fly like the wind!

June 16th

I find it difficult to concentrate at the moment. Oh, for a magic bird to bring me word from across the ocean that my Dominic has arrived on the shores of the new world; that he is safe. A letter will take as long as his own journey to reach me.

I must be patient.

June 18th

Oh, now I think I see why Juliana's being nice to me.

"We are having a neighbour of ours to dine soon," she said when she met me walking through the orchard this morning. Jack is most intelligent, and knows she dislikes him, so he keeps out of the way. (I expect there are *people* who feel as Jack does!)

"He is *very* rich," she continued, "so he is very important. You will like him."

That felt a little like an order. "Me?" I said. "What have I to do with him?"

"My mother and father wish you to join us at dinner on the last Saturday of the month."

"Me?" I said again.

"Yes, you, you goose," she said, with a silly, affected giggle.

I'm sure her parents would say that Juliana's giggle is sweet and girlish but, personally, I find it most off-putting. Why is she doing it?

June 21st

This afternoon I called Bid in from the garden to clean the curling tongs. She gets them too hot and my hair sticks and breaks off. The smell when she heats them again is revolting. As she took them, Jack barked, and I looked over Bid's shoulder to see Ned slip through the gates. I ran to meet him and hurried him inside. "Quickly! Juliana and her mother have ridden out to visit friends, and might return at any time." I was very much afraid they would, as the sky was greying, and we were clearly due for rain.

I told him about my bad thoughts when I saw him last, and apologized.

"I would never willingly bring you trouble, Mistress Susannah," he said, "and I would do all in my power to help you if you did need it."

"Oh, Ned, that is so good to hear," I said. "Isn't it, Bid?"

My maid immediately began picking singed hair off the curling tongs. "If you say so, Mistress," she said with a sniff.

Now what's the matter with her?

Ned was able to stay for a while, as it is his day off. As he and Bid and I drank ale and nibbled cold ham (from Sir Roger's kitchen), he happened to glance through the window. "Lor, Mistress, look at that weather! It's coming down like a Dartmoor waterfall!"

Indeed it was. The sky was dark and threatening. "Ned, you cannot walk all the way to the Stag's Head in this storm," I said. "Can he, Bid?"

"Course not." She used a taper to light an extra candle. "But it's late. Even if the storm passes, it'll soon be proper dark. 'Twill be dangerous being out on the roads."

Ned started to protest that he would be fine, but I said, "Bid's right. You must stay here for the night."

Her eyes went as big as boiled eggs! "*Here?* In this house?"

"Why not?" I said. "We know him well. He's hardly likely to murder us as we sleep, is he?"

"But it's not proper, Mistress, for you to have a man sleeping here."

I rolled my eyes. "Bid, you are here. You are my chaperone. And we have a spare bed – yours. Unless you wish to use it tonight, and sleep alone?"

She shivered and shook her head violently, making her cheeks wobble. I tried not to laugh, but I couldn't help it. "Then that's settled. Ned will stay here. Who knows?" I continued. "He might even catch the keeper's ghost!"

Bid squealed and buried her face in her apron. Ned just looked bewildered.

"Let's have some hot buttered ale," I suggested. "It will stop us taking cold and we—"

I was interrupted by a dreadful screeching and wailing from outside.

Bid's eyes became boiled eggs again. "The keeper!" she shrieked.

"No! It's a woman's voice!" I opened the front door and gasped. "It's Lady Anne and Juliana!"

They must have seen me silhouetted against the candlelight.

"Susannah! Let us in!" they cried.

Behind me, Bid practically threw Ned up the stairs.

The two women were drenched, their hair unpinned and their curls straggling. Bid and I dragged their cloaks off and pulled them to the kitchen fire. I rubbed Lady Anne's hands, to bring some life into them.

"Oh, cousin," she cried. "We were robbed!"

"Robbed?"

"Yes. By a highwayman!"

"A highwayman?"

"Yes, a highwayman," she snapped. Distressed as she was, she was still capable of being annoyed by me repeating her words.

Juliana had calmed down considerably and, by means of pointing and screeching, succeeded in letting Bid know that she was to remove poor Jack. Then she took over the story. They had been riding back from their friends, in good light, when the sky began to darken as the storm approached. The highwayman had been waiting in a group of no more than four or five trees…

"But he was so still, we never saw him," said Juliana.

He held them up at pistol-point and when he realized they had no money on them, he took the only ring Lady Anne was wearing, and both their necklaces.

Lady Anne burst into fresh sobs. "He s-said that as the weather was bad, he would leave us our c-clothes—"

Juliana wailed and buried her head in her damp lap.

"But he would take our mounts." Lady Anne shook her head, scattering droplets over me. "Two horses gone, cousin! *Two*! Oh, what will your father say?"

I thought it no great loss, considering they still had their lives, and said so. To my surprise both women turned on me.

"Horses do not grow on trees!"

"They cost money!"

"We cannot replace two horses just like that!" This, with a snap of Juliana's long, skinny fingers.

I bit back what I was longing to say, which was something like: Do not think that because I am poor I am nothing and that you can speak to me as you would a stable boy and that I do not have feelings. Instead I spoke gently.

"Dear cousins, do not fret so. After all, you are not poor, and…"

I broke off, shocked at their reaction. They threw themselves into each other's arms and sobbed anew.

I'd had enough. "The rain is easing," I said. "I will fetch someone to take you back to the house."

Bid was about to argue, but saw my glare. I didn't want to stay there a moment longer.

Part way along the drive, I came upon Luke, who'd been sent by Sir Roger to meet the ladies and accompany them home. I explained what had happened and he, shocked, hurried back to fetch a carriage.

I had thought all the commotion over but, as I returned to the cottage, I was amazed to see all three women rush out of the front door and hurtle up the drive towards me.

"The keeper!" screamed Bid. "'Tis the keeper!"

"Gho-o-ost!" wailed Lady Anne. "We heard its footsteps! Upstairs!"

"Run!" screeched Juliana.

I ignored them and made to walk straight past. As I did, I grasped Bid's wrist, spun her round and dragged her along behind me. She still shrieked, so I dug my nails into her wrist. "Hush, you stupid girl! You know perfectly well who it is!"

"Ow!" she cried, but she was quiet.

Lady Anne cried after me as I marched towards my front door. "Cousin! There's a ghost in there!"

I stopped and turned, hands on my hips. "That is not news to me," I said. "The keeper's ghost and I are well acquainted with each other. Goodnight."

And as I entered my cottage, I thought I heard a voice on the wind, crying, "Thank you, cousin."

But I was probably mistaken!

June 22nd

We have set up an alarm system, for when Ned is in Keeper's Cottage. Last night, under cover of darkness, Ned made a pen for Jack, in a corner of the front garden. It is bounded on two sides by hedge, and on the other two by planks of wood. Poor Ned had to nail the planks together with Bid and me over his shoulder, going, "Ssssh!" with every blow of the hammer!

The idea is that Jack will bark whenever someone comes near, and so give Ned time to run upstairs. It would be dreadful for him, and for Bid, if he were caught here. I also do not like to think what might happen to me.

June 25th

Godfrey has missed three lessons. I think he has had fear put into him by his mother and sister.

We have had much good food sent to us from the house. Pheasants, a piece of beef, some pork and two pies. It's strange, because usually I get the feeling that I am sent only those cuts from the animal that the de Gracy family rejects. The food is most welcome, however, because a dreadful thing has happened to poor Ned. He is here now, and we have heard his tale.

On the morning after the day the ladies were held up by the highwayman, Ned left early, to return to the Stag's Head. As he was leaving the boundaries of Gracy Park, he heard a cry and realized he'd been spotted by a group of men off for a day's hunting. He thought little of it until he saw that one of the men was Sir Roger.

"How I ran!" said Ned. "I didn't think I could, but I leapt

a tree stump and ran through some bushes and splashed through a stream, but I couldn't go no longer and Sir Roger caught me. He raised his whip. "Get orff my land!" he bawled. "I warned you! I don't want oafs like you anywhere near my wife and children. Gorn! Gorn! Gettorff!"

Bid looked upset. "He hurt you bad?"

Ned nodded. "He whipped me till I reached the river. But Kate MacPhee took care of me. She's a good woman, so don't you say nothing against her, will you?"

I was puzzled. "Why should we do that?"

Ned hung his head. "Because I lost my job. Sykes MacPhee, he came to me this morning, and he seemed truly sorry."

"Sorry for what?"

"He said he had no choice. He had to let me go. Mistress Susannah, I think it's Sir Roger's doing. He's making sure I can't get work anywhere near Gracy Park."

I think so, too. I am so angry. But I can do nothing. Nothing except offer Ned shelter. The poor boy has nowhere else to go, so Bid and I will help him. She, the dear girl, offered for Ned to stay at her mother's cottage, down in the village, but I would not get Bid's family into trouble for all the world. Ned, himself, says that no one would dare harbour him, for fear of Sir Roger's wrath. Well, I dare. My brother would not have Ned sleep under a hedge, not while he could give him shelter. Dominic is not here, so I am right that I do this.

Strange that Bid did not argue so much this time. Perhaps she sees the value of having a man, however lame, in the house. She certainly didn't hear the keeper's ghost last time Ned stayed – at least not after the two ladies' adventure!

June 27th

Our alarm system has worked well all week, except for yesterday, when Godfrey came for a lesson. He brought a bone for my little dog. Jack knows Godfrey so well, and he must have smelled the bone. It completely took his attention and he forgot to bark.

Poor Godfrey has been unwell – spotty, in fact. His mother feared it was the measles, but the rash went quickly, and there was no fever. He didn't mention his mother's encounter with the so-called ghost, but he did say she didn't want him to come any more. However, his father says he may – but only if our lessons are held with the front door wide open, and he is to run if anything disturbs him.

Since we had no warning of Godfrey's arrival, poor Ned spent the next hour or so listening to him and me speaking French while he was huddled on the kitchen floor under a mountain of dirty clothes and bed sheets.

Bid said afterwards, "I was afraid he'd fall asleep and start snoring, so I had to keep kicking him!"

"I didn't mind," said Ned.

I am glad that those two get on well. I was afraid they would squabble, or that Bid would give him away to Sir Roger.

Oh horrors! I've just remembered. Tomorrow is the day I go to dine with the family and their rich neighbour. I shall hate it. And what am I to wear?

June 28th

Thank goodness Bid sews well. She has worked wonders, taking ribbon from this, and lace from that, and put a bow here and a tuck there, and I shall really look quite presentable at dinner. When she has finished and everything is pressed with the iron, she is to curl my hair. I want the curls so tight that they will not droop as I make my way to the house. Or should I saddle Moonbeam and ride? I think I will. Side-saddle, of course!

Much later

Well, goodness me, late though it is, I must describe the neighbour, Sir Staveney Vean. He is ancient – at least fifty – and the most peculiar shape: long and thin, but with a bulging, well-stuffed stomach, and a large head. It looks too big for his body. His arms and legs are long and thin, and if he had two more, he would resemble a giant grey ant. His clothes were rich, much richer than Sir Roger's, and his periwig must have been in the latest London style, for he made Sir Roger look positively drab by comparison.

I curtsied on being introduced. He took my hand, kissed it with dry, cracked lips and muttered, "Dedoooo." I gathered this was his version of "How do you do?"

I was placed opposite Sir Staveney at dinner, and had the pleasure of watching Juliana simpering. She seems to admire him greatly. I do not. I found his habit of staring at me most disconcerting, and I also found Lady Anne's attentions quite peculiar. She seemed falsely bright, and frequently drew me into the conversation, which was most courteous of her, but when I had spoken, all talk from them suddenly ceased while Sir Staveney stared at me again.

Once, when there was a lull in the conversation, Sir Staveney leaned forward across the table. He is so long and thin that I quite thought he was after something on my plate – he could certainly have reached it. But no.

"So, me dear, all alone in the world, heh?"

"Not at all, sir," I said. "I have a brother."

"A brother?" he said in surprised tones. "Do you now? Then where is he? Demned if I can see him. Is he under the table, heh?" And he burst out laughing. I could clearly see his half-chewed beef, hooked on a side tooth. I would like to have knocked the tooth out.

Lady Anne broke in. "Dear cousin Susannah is staying with us while her brother ventures to the new world," she said. "America!"

"Indeed." Sir Staveney stared at me again. "Then, me dear, you are certainly alone in *this* world, what? Heh! Heh, heh!"

Juliana laughed so much I thought she might split the bones in her bodice. No, I *hoped* she would.

The time dragged, and I was mightily relieved when Lady Anne indicated that the ladies should go and sit comfortably while the men attended to their wine. It is a mark of how repulsive I found Sir Staveney that I was pleased to go and make small talk on a couch with Juliana while her mother stitched tapestry in extremely ugly colours. Juliana was in a quite teasing mood, which I found very off-putting.

"So, Susan, have you considered whom you might one day marry?"

"Of course not," I replied. "I am too young and know few men. And I have no wish to marry. When my—"

"Yes, we know, cousin," said Lady Anne. "We know you think to wait for your brother. But . . ." she put down her grey and brown wools and gazed into space, with one finger to her chin – a very false pose in my opinion. "I wonder if it might not be a good idea for you at least to consider the idea."

"I thank you, but I will not," I replied. Firm, but polite, I thought and felt rather pleased with myself. They, however, were not pleased with me. Juliana got up and flounced over to sit beside her mother. From that moment, they addressed scarcely a word to me.

Good.

I was relieved when Sir Staveney asked for his carriage. I was about to ask if Luke could bring Moonbeam to the door and if Bid could be fetched from the kitchen, where she'd spent the evening, when Sir Roger almost hustled Sir Staveney past me. Lady Anne pulled me back and kept hold of my wrist. Only when Sir Staveney had left was I able to request Moonbeam.

Is it mean of me to think that the de Gracy family don't wish it to be known that they are boarding their cousin in a supposedly ghost-ridden old cottage?

Now we are home and we are all warm and comfortable.

Bid already snuffles beside me, and Ned is snoring in her bedroom. I know he is, for I can hear him. He is stuffed full of good food, because Bid smuggled a whole apronful back with her. She walked alongside (she refuses to mount Moonbeam behind me) as I rode elegantly, side-saddle, with half a leg of mutton balanced on my pommel.

July 8th

Poor Ned goes quietly mad cooped up in the cottage all the time. He has mended everything that needs mending, and has taken to delving in the keeper's hoard to see if he can make or mend anything there. I have asked him to remove anything that smells or that might smell, and Bid often has a great bonfire. Anything that will not burn and that is useless is being buried in a pit that Ned dug under cover of darkness. He is becoming quite a night owl. He has permission, whenever he wishes, to muffle Moonbeam's hooves with rags (thank you, keeper!) and to walk him out of Gracy Park, where he may then have a fine ride!

July 11th

Jack is the best and cleverest dog in all the world.

Today Ned asked if he could bathe, as it is halfway through the year, and Bid immediately fetched the tub, and they began filling it between them.

"This will be the first warm bath I've had for a long time," he said. "At the Stag's Head, I used the horses' trough to wash my hands. The water was full of strings of slime, so I had to keep going down to the river after work to wash the stink off."

"Give me your clothes," said Bid, "and I'll wash them. You can wrap yourself in a blanket until they're dry. It won't be long. There's a strong breeze."

I had a bright idea. "Ned, I have some breeches you may borrow. They are Dominic's. Bid, you know where they are, I'm sure. Fetch them for Ned, please."

She went upstairs, clattered about and soon returned. "Mistress, is your brother a very *small* man?"

"No. Why?"

She held up the breeches.

Ned burst out laughing. Of course they were small. They were the ones I wore on that night when…

My eyes filled at the memory. "Put them away, Bid. Dominic was much younger when he wore those."

She looked inside. "They look as if he stitched them himself."

I ignored her. Soon Ned was enjoying a warm bath, his clothes were spread on the currant bushes near the kitchen door, and Bid and I were sipping cups of chocolate, which she had brought from the big house. Such luxury! Suddenly, Jack barked. I rushed to the window. "Lady Anne, Sir Roger, Juliana – they're all coming!"

In seconds, Bid had dragged Ned's clothes out of sight, Ned himself had run dripping and naked (I did not look) up the stairs, and I had thrust the chocolate cups behind the little log pile.

For once I was glad Juliana was with them, for it meant that the de Gracys wouldn't enter the garden until I had removed Jack. This gave Bid and Ned precious extra moments.

Once they were in, Lady Anne cast her eyes around. "There is water on your stairs, cousin," she said. "If you have a leak, we will be glad to send a man to fix it."

"No, no, I thank you. It was only Bid, taking her bath."

They glanced towards the closed kitchen door but, thankfully, did not enquire further.

I invited them to sit down.

"We are enjoying a little exercise in the fresh air," said

Sir Roger, "and decided to call on you and make sure that all is well."

"All is very well, I thank you."

"Are you not lonely here, Susan?" asked Juliana.

I decided not to correct her misuse of my name. "Lonely? No! I have Bid, and Godfrey comes for his lessons, and I have Jack." Goodness, was she going to offer to keep me company?

"But still, it is nice to have a companion, of one's own class."

Lord, I thought, please don't say Juliana wants me for her companion.

Sir Roger humphed. "Errk, hmm. Of course, if you were to have a gentleman pay you his attentions, that would not go amiss, I presume?"

I smiled. I truly did not know what to say. What were they talking about?

We spoke a little more, then they got up to go. Lady Anne leaned forward to kiss the air beside my cheek. "Do come and drink tea with us tomorrow afternoon at three," she said.

"Errk, hmm. Might be someone there who wishes to talk to you."

"Goodbye, cousin."

"Goodbye, Susan."

"Errk. Yes."

I closed the door behind them, freed Jack, called, "They've

gone!" and collapsed on a stool. I wondered at the visit. All most peculiar.

And then, as if a hammer had descended on my head, it hit me. All the marriage talk. Sir Staveney. They were talking about Sir Staveney. He wishes to talk to me.

"No!" I cried.

Bid came rushing in. "What is it, Mistress?"

"Sir Staveney wants to marry me!"

Bid made a face. "Ugh, no! Oh, Mistress, no. Say it isn't true!"

Ned put his head round the door. "I can't come in. I only got this blanket round me. Did I hear right, Mistress?"

"I fear it's so, Ned."

"Bid told me all about Sir Staveney. You can't marry him."

"I'm afraid they might force me. I am in Sir Roger's care."

Ned pulled his blanket tighter and edged into the room. "Mistress, if you was already married, you could not marry Sir Staveney."

"But I am not, and I know no one—"

Ned pulled himself as straight as he could. "Mistress, I would marry you if it would save you from that man."

Bless his good heart. I would not hurt his feelings for the world, and I was saved from doing so by Bid.

"You will do no such thing, Ned Allin. There might be another as'd want to marry you, so you better not go throwing yourself away."

And she stormed from the room.

Looking back, I realize that dear Ned had no idea what Bid was saying. But I had.

Now I must face tomorrow. Dare I refuse? What would happen if I did?

And for goodness' sake, why would Sir Staveney want to marry me? I have nothing to bring to the marriage – nothing except my connection to the de Gracy family.

Is that it? Is Sir Staveney a common man by birth? A common man who has made great wealth and now wishes to move high in the social world?

Are the de Gracys perhaps not as wealthy as I thought? I remember the slightly shabby furniture and hangings, the ladies' distress over the theft of two horses. Is this intended as a marriage of convenience? Sir Staveney's wealth to join with the de Gracy family name – their social standing? Then why does he not marry Juliana? Perhaps Sir Roger is not that desperate. Perhaps he isn't prepared to sacrifice his daughter, but would willingly "sell" a poor cousin. Oh, so many questions.

July 12th

Oh, what have I done? What is to become of me?

I was the first guest to arrive at the big house. The family were so pleased to see me, they practically stroked me.

"Now, cousin Susannah," said Sir Roger.

I waited.

"Errk, hmm. If someone should wish to speak privately with you, I trust you will not object."

I decided to be ignorant. "But who would wish to speak with me?"

"Well, er…"

Juliana leaned forward, a knowing smile on her face. At least, I imagine it was intended to be a smile. To me it was little more than a smirk.

I was saved from further discussion by the arrival of Sir Staveney. He sat in the master's chair by the fireplace and his eyes immediately went to me.

I waited, my heart in my mouth, wondering how on earth I would deal with his romantic advances. Not that I could imagine this tall, grey, ant-like man being even remotely romantic.

The conversation continued around me and I lost myself in a wonderful daydream, in which I looked out of the window beside me and saw a scarlet-and-gold carriage draw up. From it leapt a fine young man, who removed his feathered hat and swept a deep bow. Only when he looked up at me did I see that it was my brother.

"You smile, Mistress Makepeace!" said Sir Staveney. "You look well when you have a pleased expression."

"Errk, hmm," said Sir Roger. "We may hope to see that expression more often very soon, may we not, Sir Staveney?" And he winked.

It was coming! Sir Staveney was going to propose. I panicked and leapt to my feet!

"Forgive me!" I cried. "I am unwell!"

And I ran from the room. From the house. I did not stop running until I had turned a bend in the drive and could no longer be seen. Tears of frustration and anger poured down my face. How could they think to let me go – to *sell* me – to that horrible man!

I reached home and was much comforted by Ned and Bid. They are such good friends. I have asked them both to call me Susannah, but they find it difficult. They will get used to it, I'm sure. It has been hard not to be called simply by my name. I am called either Mistress Susannah, cousin Susannah, or the hateful Susan.

Ned is indignant, and insists that I cannot be forced to

marry. I suppose if I scream and shout they might find it not worth their while to force me. But what would happen to me if I anger Sir Roger so much that he decides to throw me out? And what would happen to Ned and Bid? And my poor Jack? Ohhh!

July 19th

Almost a week has gone by and I am called to the house again. Will that awful man be there?

Later

Sir Staveney was indeed there and, thankfully, I think he has left behind the idea of marriage to me. He brought his son and it was a much livelier gathering than before. In fact, I almost enjoyed it, because Master Dunby Vean is so supremely stupid. I do not mean that there is something wrong with him, that he is simple. No, I think not. He is just very vain and stupid.

But he served my purpose, because I chose to speak much with Dunby Vean and to laugh like a silly little girl at his silly little jokes, all to spite Sir Staveney. And I think it worked, for Sir Staveney watched me like a cat watches a butterfly, his bony face twitching and his eyes darting after me.

The only thing about Dunby Vean that interested me was that he has a four-year-old daughter called Elvina. Elvina Vean. Whatever was her foolish father thinking of? Dunby's wife is dead, and I feel so sorry for Elvina, for not only is she motherless, but she has a clot for a father. Sir Staveney adores her, that much was clear from the way his hard face softened when the child was mentioned. That is the first time I have thought of him as human.

I even seem to have been forgiven by the family, who were all most pleasant. So that all seems to be sorted out, and I can go back to my dull little life again. My life of waiting for the man I really do care about. Dominic.

July 24th

My heart aches so, and I do not know what to think. Godfrey ran in yesterday while Bid and I were topping and tailing gooseberries for a pie. We had little warning but, thank goodness, Ned was burrowing in the keeper's hoard of junk and Bid flew out and shut the door on him.

"A letter! A letter!" Godfrey shouted, waving it at me. "Is it from America? From your brother?"

"Oh, it is sure to be," I said, wiping my hands on my bodice. I was shaking with excitement.

"To Mistress Susannah Makepeace," it said. "From Hannah Carew.

"Mistress Makepeace, I am sorry to rite with bad news of yore brother, who is sick. Me and my man are doing our best to care for him but we have six children and it is difficult he has been sick since he came on the ship from England which is not many days past. He had a fall on board and hurt his leg bad. There is fever on him. Yore brother needs someone to look after him all the time and I have too much to do with the animals and growing our food. Many people have been sick and all have there problems but if you send some money I will find a good widow woman to nurse yore brother and grow food. His leg will never be right, I fear. It is mending badly. He needs more doctoring than I can give him. Even if he gets well tomorrow which he will not he will be weak and he won't be strong enough to do the hard work we have to do just to stay alive. Out here, them as can't work, dies and with his leg, it won't be easy for him even when he's fit and well, which he will be one day God willing.

"I promise I will do all I can to make him better but I pray you send him money. I will look after him until I hear from you, do not fear, but I pray you be quick, for all our sakes.

"Yours in faith, Hannah Carew."

There followed the name of the place where they live but I could not read it, I was weeping so.

Godfrey, bless him, had gone. Bid released Ned and they came to me, and we all shed a tear.

"Will you send money?" asked Bid.

"I must," I said, "but I have hardly any."

My dear friends pooled all they had, but between us, there was scarcely enough to feed a man for two days.

I spent the best part of an hour curled up on my bed, wondering how I could raise money. And then the answer came to me. I sat up.

"Bid! Ned!"

They hurried to me.

"Listen!" I said. "In the time it takes for money to reach Dominic, I can be there myself. I will go to him. I will nurse him! Oh, hurry, I must get ready. Will I be in time?" I began to rush around frenziedly, picking up things and throwing them down again.

"Mistress!" said Bid, but I took no notice. "Mistress Susannah! You're like a bluebottle trapped in a hot room. Stop. Think. You would need money to get to America."

I calmed myself.

Bid took my hands. "I've heard Ned's story about how him and your brother were going to sail together. It was not having money that sent Ned back here."

"And glad I am that he came," I said, "but Bid—"

"Mistress," she said gently. "You cannot go without money."

I pulled away from her. "Then I will get money. Somehow I will!"

And now, after a night spent throwing myself around the bed, I sit at my pear-wood table, my mind in turmoil. I must go to Dominic. Good Hannah Carew is clearly prepared to care for Dominic until money reaches them so, instead of a purse, she will receive me.

Oh, here is Godfrey again. I suppose he wants his French lesson. My heart is not in it. I shall tell him to go and play with Jack, who speaks French perfectly.

Later

I was wrong. Godfrey came to tell me to get myself ready, as the de Gracy carriage was being sent for me. Bid and I flew round, preparing my clothes and hair, and for once I am perfectly willing to visit the family. For I have a plan. I will throw myself on their mercy, and ask them to lend me some money, until such time as I return from America and can repay them. For repay them I will.

There, I thought. My problem is solved.

The carriage duly arrived and I was taken to the house. There I found Sir Staveney with Sir Roger, and no sign at all of Lady Anne or Juliana – except for a slight movement I spotted through the parlour door, which was not quite shut.

"Sir Roger?" I said.

"Your presence is required in the parlour," he replied.

A footman opened the door and I was ushered in. I fully expected to find the ladies in there, so I was greatly surprised to discover Dunby Vean.

"Master Vean?" I felt uncomfortable at being alone with him.

He giggled. "Yes, Mistress, it is I. If not I, who else could I be?"

I couldn't bring myself to giggle like him – I am not an idiot – so I smiled. But Dunby Vean seemed to take my smile for pleasure at his so-called wit.

"Mistress Makepeace. Susannah," he said. "Oh, wait a moment. I forgot. Sit down."

He was jigging about from one foot to the other so I thought he might calm down if I obeyed. But when I was seated, he came charging towards me and threw himself down on one knee.

"Father told me this is the way to do it," he said, with a demented grin. "Susannah Makepeace, will you marry me?"

I gaped at him. He leapt up, jigged around the room, and laughed aloud. "There! I've done it! I'm engaged!"

I'd recovered my own wits by then. "Sir, you most certainly are not engaged. At least, not to me." And I swept from the room. My sweeping was spoiled however by the gaggle of people outside the door, who'd clearly been eavesdropping. I knew they had by the expressions on their faces.

"How *could* you…?" I was almost in tears.

"How could we what?" Lady Anne spoke icily.

"I thought you wanted me to marry *him*," I said rudely, stabbing a finger at Sir Staveney. "I thought you'd realized I wouldn't, and I thought you were accepting of that."

"Errk, hmm. It seems to me you thought too much, young woman," said Sir Roger.

Sir Staveney was beyond speech.

Dunby spoke, from behind me. "She turned me down, Father. Can we go home now? I've got a rum new puppy I'm itching to train for the hunt."

"See?" I said. "Even that – that… Even *Dunby* couldn't care less. Neither of us wants to marry."

Juliana had been steaming quietly behind her mother. Now she came forward. "You ungrateful wretch. Why couldn't you do this one thing for us, after all we've done for you?"

I shook my head. "I don't understand. I don't understand why it's so important to you. I don't understand why you all *care* so much."

I cared. I felt used. I was about to cry, but I will *never* do that in front of the de Gracy family. I bobbed a very shallow curtsey and fled.

Now I know why Juliana wasn't considered for marriage. Even she wouldn't stoop to marry such an empty-headed clodpoll as Dunby Vean. But they thought their poor cousin Susannah might!

At least the proposal took my mind off my brother's predicament for an hour. But as soon as I got back, I forgot the proposal and fell to thinking about what I can do. One certain thing is that I am going to Dominic, somehow, and the other certain thing is that I need money.

I shall ask Bid to take what I do not need and sell it for me.

July 26th

Ned has spent much time sorting through the keeper's things and trying to make or mend. He has made a small stool. It is really fit only for milking, as the legs are short and I cannot get down gracefully to sit on it! He has gathered pieces of gun and put a pistol back together again. I think he could sell that, but he says he'd rather keep it for now.

"Why?" I asked.

He shrugged.

Hmm. I know Ned well and I feel he is up to something.

Bid has "borrowed" two more of Juliana's books, and two silver spoons which somehow slipped into the rubbish. Though how she saw them, and no one else did is beyond me. She has asked Ned to take them to the Stag's Head.

"You'll surely find a buyer there," she said.

"I will," said Ned.

"Take the pistol," I suggested. "Some highwayman might be glad of it. Please, Ned. I need the money, and I do not like to have guns in the house."

He eyed me. "Perhaps I should become a highwayman

myself, Mistress Susannah. I might get enough in one night for you to go to America."

I laughed. But he didn't.

July 28th

Ned went out to check his rabbit traps last night, and this morning he stayed long abed. I almost forgot about him until halfway through Godfrey's lesson, when there were creaks from above.

Godfrey's face paled. "It's the keeper," he breathed. "Come, cousin, let's get out of here."

"Don't be such a poopnoddy, Godfrey. There's no ghost. How many times must I tell you?"

But my own blood chilled in my veins at the sound of a long-drawn-out, ghostly wail from the room above, then more creaks and thumps.

"Bid?" I cried.

She didn't come to me. Why didn't she come?

There was another wail, as if someone was in torment. I panicked. Had Ned come home at all last night? Had something happened to him? Where was Bid? Were Godfrey and I alone in the cottage – with a ghost?

"Quick!" I grabbed Godfrey's hand and we ran outside. Jack jumped up at me, but he didn't seem afraid. Godfrey did! He flung the front gate open and sped along the drive.

"I'm never going in there again!" he cried.

I leaned against the gate. My breath was rapid, and I felt chilled through. Although I dreaded what I might see, I raised my eyes to the upstairs window.

Looking down at me were two stupid grinning faces.

"You fools!" I cried. "You scared me to death. And look at poor Godfrey."

They couldn't, because he was out of sight.

I berated my silly servant, and told Ned he should know better than to frighten a child, but he had an answer for me.

"Mistress Susannah, Bid and I think you shouldn't teach that Master Godfrey no more. They treated you too harshly. We hated seeing you so upset as you was when you came back the other day."

"Oh, you've messed up my plan," I cried. "I've made up my mind to ask them for help. The family think little of me as it is. If Godfrey won't come to me for lessons any more, they'll think even less." Bid and Ned looked so upset at my outburst that my heart softened instantly. "Oh, bless you for caring so much about me," I said, "but I must give them no more cause to despise me. I truly need their help."

"You're going to ask them for money?"

"For a loan, Bid. I will borrow the money to go to America

– they will be glad to see me gone. And then you can go back and work in the big house, and Ned, you must take anything you wish from the keeper's hoard and, of course, Moonbeam. Please try not to sell him, but if you have to, then so be it."

Bid looked at Ned. Ned looked at Bid.

"Tell her," said Bid.

Ned swallowed. "Mistress, you must not lower yourself to ask for money from they de Gracy folk. I'll get you money."

"You? But how?" I looked from one to the other. "Oh no!"

"I can do it," said Ned. "I got a pistol. I can be a highwayman. All you have to do is point the gun and say something like, 'Hold!' or 'Stand fast!' and then take what they got."

I couldn't believe what I was hearing. "And then you have to get away, Ned. How can you? You are used to riding a steady old horse. I know you've ridden Moonbeam, just for pleasure, but he's a powerful animal. You need strong legs to manage a horse like that at full gallop." I shook my head. "If your victim raised the alarm or gave chase, you would be caught. I cannot let you do it."

Bid put a large meat pasty in front of us. "I'm glad. I told you, Ned, you wasn't to do it, and the mistress says you can't, so you can't."

I laughed. "But I might! How would that be? Highway girl!"

We all laughed then, and toasted each other in beer. How lucky I am to have these good people around me.

The pasty was delicious.

Later

I cannot believe we had a serious conversation about robbing people. What have I come to?

Tomorrow morning I will go and ask for my loan.

July 29th

Bid is very tight-lipped this morning. She doesn't want me to go to the de Gracy family and beg for money. I'm grateful that she thinks of me, but it makes me cross. Does she not realize that I would do anything rather than beg. But how else can I get money quickly?

Yes, I could marry that revolting twerp, Dunby.

Advantages

1. Money
2. I could be a good mother to his poor little daughter, Elvina
3. I wouldn't be dependent on the de Gracy family
4. They would have to treat me with respect

Disadvantages

1. A vain halfwit for a husband
2. A harsh, cold-hearted insect of a father-in-law
3. If I ran off to America I would bring disgrace on my relations
4. If I ran off to America I would be letting down that poor little child
5. If I fell in love with someone else – a real man – I could never marry him and be happy

No. It must be a loan. Now I just have to pluck up courage. Maybe I could take the pistol Ned put together and point it at them. "Lend me some money," I could say. "Your money or your daughter's life!" Ha!

Later

Well, I went. I showed them the letter, and they were very sympathetic.

"I wouldn't worry, cousin," said Lady Anne. "These Carew people don't sound the sort to just throw a man out to starve. They will look after him."

"But you don't understand," I said. "It is a hard life in America. There are no shops or markets. They must chop down trees to build their homes, they must grow everything from seed... Nothing is easy."

Juliana shrugged and made her thin lips go even thinner. One day they'll disappear and she'll look like a stuffed scarecrow's head.

"None of us finds life easy, Susan."

I could not believe she'd spoken those words. She lives in a fine house. Yes, the furnishings are somewhat shabby, but she has servants, and enough to eat, and they are all well and warmly dressed. They think they are hard up, yet they don't know what real hardship is.

But I kept these thoughts to myself. I took a deep breath and asked my favour. When I'd finished speaking, there was a short silence. Then Lady Anne spoke.

"My dear, are you quite mad?" She turned to Sir Roger. "She cannot go, can she?"

"Indeed no," he said gruffly. "Errk, hmm. If I let you go, cousin, I should be failing in my duty."

I spoke quietly. "Sir, I should be failing in mine if I did not go." I tried one last appeal. "Please. Help me. Lend me the money."

Juliana jumped to her feet. "Money! Haven't you had enough? You *cost* us money! Why—"

Thankfully, Sir Roger silenced her. If she had gone on, I think I would have slapped her.

I got to my feet. "I thank you for your time. I will not trouble you again."

They stood, and Lady Anne took my arm and walked me to the open door. "Go back to your little cottage," she said. "Sit and wait and trust that all will be well. For I'm sure it will be."

I set off, but she called to me from the window. "Susannah! Wait!"

I turned, a shiver of hope running through me. Had they changed their minds?

"Godfrey would prefer you to come here for his lessons. Tomorrow, then?"

I didn't trust myself to speak, but came straight home to record my thoughts.

Oh, Jack is barking. Someone is coming.

Dusk

My visitor was Juliana.

"I have had such a good idea to help you get to America!" she said. "I had to come straight away to tell you."

"Oh, cousin, thank you!" I cried, regretting that I'd ever doubted her character. "You'll help me, then?"

I assumed she would offer me something I could sell, but how wrong could I be?

"Well, of course, I cannot help you personally," she said. "I have nothing of my own, you know."

Liar. They may have fallen on slightly harder times, but they have plenty.

"No, this is my idea," she said. "One of our servants left us to emigrate, and he had nothing at all. Even less than you!"

"Then how did he travel?"

"Simple," she said. "What you do is this. You agree to work on a plantation for a fixed time, and the plantation owner pays for your board and passage across the ocean. You see?"

"Work? As what?"

"As a servant, of course." She looked uneasy as she saw my expression, and well she might. "Cousin, you have little choice. Er, I can see you do not like my idea." She backed away. "I do assure you I meant well."

"Thank you for sparing precious time to think of me, cousin Juliana," I said. "It is getting dark. You should go home."

I could have added, "Before I slap your face," but I did not.

Luke was waiting for her, of course. That girl thinks she is poor but she has everything she needs. Everything I do not have.

One thing I do know. I will find that money. I will! I don't care how. And I will do whatever is necessary to get me on that ship to America.

July 31st

Two nights have passed. I have not slept. I toss and turn, and kick Bid to stop her snorting. I listen to the owls. I count chickens in a chicken run. But I cannot sleep. Something terrible, but exciting, is going through my mind. I cannot bring myself to write the words, though there is no one in this cottage who can read.

August 1st

Tonight!

August 2nd

All morning yesterday, I prepared. I sorted my clothes out. I gave Ned extra food – feed – for Moonbeam. I gathered rags. I took a couple of handfuls of damp soil and put them inside a little blue pouch – an old silk one that has seen better days. I found a reasonably clean sack and hid it in the stable.

Then I reminisced in front of Bid about my mother, and we both shed a little tear. I told her I could not see my mother, but she could see hers whenever she wanted.

"Go!" I said. "Go today, Bid. Perhaps it is an omen that we are talking of your mother. Perhaps she needs you. Maybe she's unwell."

"Oh, don't say that, Mistress. You makes me feel bad."

"Then go to her."

"But time's a-moving on. I would never get back afore dark, and you know I don't like the dark."

"Stay with her, Bid. I will be perfectly all right. I have Ned here, and I shall forbid him to go out rabbiting."

And she did. Ned and I waved her off, with her arms full of little gifts for her mother (by courtesy of the de Gracy kitchen and garden).

"You are kind, Mistress Susannah," said Ned.

Oh yes?

I was extra generous during the late afternoon and early evening. I sat sewing while the light held, and kept Ned supplied with strong ale, and then plenty of good wine. He always sleeps well, but I knew that what he was drinking would make him sleep through the loudest thunderstorm. Before long, I was helping him up to Bid's little room. I let him roll on to the bed, then closed the shutters and crept out.

I went to my bedroom and changed my clothes. Can it be six months since I last wore Dominic's breeches? I took out the hat I'd worn that night we left home – the very hat I'd pulled low over my face when we met the highwayman.

I would be pulling it low again but, this time, I would be the highwayman.

I gave Jack the heel of a loaf of bread to chew on and told him to be quiet. Then I crept out to Moonbeam's makeshift stable. I wrapped and tied rags round his hooves so that I could get him off de Gracy land with the least chance of being heard. Once saddled, I led him out and along the drive. I was ready to pull him into the shrubbery if I heard the slightest sound of anyone coming.

We made it through the gates with no problem, other than me jumping in fright as a badger scuttled across our path. The road beyond Gracy Park is little more than a track, and I headed for the crossroads, about a mile away. There, I turned right and, where the woods grew close, I urged Moonbeam into the trees. Once we were among the shadows, I pulled out my afternoon's sewing – a black mask which covered my eyes and the upper part of my face. I reached into the blue silk pouch, which I'd tied to the saddle, and took out the damp dirt. I rubbed this around my face. I have seen how white owls gleam in the darkness, and I didn't want my cheeks and chin to do the same.

I waited and waited. It must have been nigh on two hours.

Down in the valley to my right, candles glimmered in several windows of a rambling building, and in the moonlight I could make out smoke curling lazily upwards.

Sometimes I saw movement, people going in and out and silhouetted for a moment against the lamplight in the doorway. Sometimes the sound of harsh voices floated up to me. The Stag's Head. Just beyond it was a double bridge. The first arch went over a river, the second over a stream that ran parallel to it. The water gleamed silver in the moonlight. Ned told me he caught our trout in that stream.

No one came.

Oh, well, I thought. That's that. Susannah Makepeace, highway girl. That's a laugh. And I rode home with my pathetic empty sack, half disappointed that I was none the richer for my night's work, and half relieved that I hadn't been forced to rob anyone.

For that is how I'm thinking now. I will be forced to do it. There is no other way I can get to my brother before it's too late.

I finally fell into bed, and then could not sleep. My thoughts were all imaginings of what it will be like when I get to America. I will nurse Dominic back to health – I will, I will. Then we will build ourselves a home and we will both work the land, and when we are rich, we'll come home, and I'll find Bid and Ned, and we'll pay our debts and all will be well. All will be well. That was my final thought as I fell asleep.

My first thought as I woke this morning made my skin go cold and clammy, my heart pound and my blood run hot. I must have a guardian angel, I really must. I have called Dunby Vean stupid, but none come more stupid than me.

I dressed as a highwayman, and waited for my first victim, and I didn't have a pistol! I completely forgot to take it!

Tonight will be different.

Later

Ned knows. He knows because I left too many clues. I really am a dunderhead. I left the rag bindings on Moonbeam's hooves. I left my blue silk pouch tied to the saddle (I did at least think to take that off, so poor Moonbeam could get some rest). And when I came downstairs to get a drink this morning, Ned was sitting at the table, his head in his hands, moaning about how he'd drunk too much, and never again and all that. Then he looked up at me, and his eyes widened in surprise.

"Mistress, you're filthy. What's happened?"

I had forgotten to rub my disguise off my face. Once he put that together with the trail of clues I'd left, there was the most almighty row. It only ended when I told Ned, rather nastily, to remember his place and watch how he spoke to me. I feel bad about that.

I told him that being a highway girl is easy and safe. "I've proved it, haven't I? I'm back here, safe and sound."

"So who did you rob? And what did you get?"

That foxed me. I thought quickly. "I did not really intend to rob anyone last night. It was just a practice, to see if I can do it. And I can!"

"Who did you see on the road?" He looked hard at me.

I felt that the word "liar" was scrawled across my forehead. Then I remembered that he could not read it even if it was, and I pushed on with my lies.

"Oh, all manner of people. Coaches, men on horseback, a lady in a fine carriage..."

"You didn't see no one, did you?"

I was about to insist that I did when I saw how pointless it is to lie. "No one."

He laughed! "That's because you went too late!"

"When should I have gone?"

"Either twilight, when foolish people are still travelling, or after nightfall, at the time men are making their way home from the inn. Oh, sometimes you might get someone who's travelling all night, but that's generally 'cos they haven't got the price of a bed. They ain't worth robbing."

I set some cold mutton and the remains of yesterday's bread before him. "Ned. Help me. Support me. I have to do this."

"Mistress, why won't you let me do it?"

"You cannot. You are lame; you could not control Moonbeam at full speed. And think! If you were thrown, how would you escape on foot?"

He hung his head.

"No," I said. "It's impossible. It must be me. I go again tonight. Will you help me?"

Slowly, he nodded.

Just then, Bid came in. "Morning, you two. Goodness, why the long faces? Juliana de Gracy hasn't been here, has she?" Bid is always worried my cousin will notice the books that find their way to my shelf.

Ned looked up at me. "Tell her."

I couldn't believe my ears. "*What?*"

"Tell Bid. Or I will. I don't keep no secrets from her."

Clearly their friendship has deepened. I have been too wrapped up in my own thoughts to notice.

"You tell her," I said. "I'm taking Jack for a walk. I need to clear my head. As do you," I added sharply to Ned.

August 3rd

I did it. I went again. Ned has persuaded Bid to keep my secret, and I have promised them that part of anything I ~~steal~~ acquire shall be theirs, so that when I go to America, they will have something of their own. For they won't have this cottage and, anyway, Ned couldn't stay hidden all his life.

How long he can stay hidden at all is a problem. For while I was off walking with Jack, they didn't have their sentry to let them know of visitors. Poor Ned had to dive under the kitchen table when Juliana knocked on the door. She had brought me some sewing to do, to while away the time. Not embroidery, or tapestry. Oh no! She brought two of her old gowns for me to wear, but asked me to remove the lace trimmings and return them to her so she could have them put on a new gown. It's a wonder she didn't ask me to do that for her, too!

Anyway, dusk found me once again hidden among some tall trees. This time I knew I had someone waiting for me at home. And this time, I had a pistol. I cannot shoot anyone, as Ned couldn't get all the parts for the firing mechanism, but it looks most threatening. Thank you, keeper! And this time, Moonbeam's face was as dirty as mine. Ned pointed out how the moonbeam marking was so distinctive.

"He'd be recognized in a trice by someone local," he said.

"But nobody sees him. I don't go anywhere, do I?"

Ned rolled his eyes. "The de Gracy family see him. Their servants see him. Maybe even their friends see him. And anyway," he continued impatiently, "someone's only got to say they was robbed by someone riding a horse with *moonbeam* markings on its face..."

Ned had a point. I did as he said.

Once I was in the trees – in a different place this time – I scarcely had to wait more than a few minutes. A horse and rider came trotting along the road. They moved so fast there was barely a moment to think. I pulled my hat down low over my piled-up hair, checked my mask was in place, took up the pistol and urged Moonbeam to the edge of the road. I trembled badly, but I just kept thinking, Dominic, Dominic, Dominic…

At first I thought the rider hadn't seen me, but I think he was paralysed with shock.

"Hold, there!" I growled.

He yanked on his reins, and the horse stopped.

"What d'you want? I've got nothing, I tell you!"

"Give me your money!" I gestured with the pistol towards a bag hanging from his saddle. "And that!"

He unhooked the bag and tossed it to the ground in front of my horse.

"And your money! Be quick about it! I know you have money!"

He fished around and I heard the clank of coins. These he flung to the ground, too. "That's all I've got, I swear. Let me go. I've got little ones at home awaiting their father. Think of the little ones."

I didn't really take in what he was saying. I was wondering what to do next. I couldn't get off Moonbeam and pick up the money, in case he jumped on me, so I waved the pistol again. "Go! Fast as you can. And don't look back, or it'll be the worse for you."

He didn't need telling twice. "Thank you. Thank you." And he was gone.

I waited a moment, hoping no one else would appear,

and made sure he didn't look back. Then I dismounted and grabbed the bag and all the coins and stuffed them in my sack. Within half a minute Moonbeam and I were on our way home.

It seems as if I did all this coolly and calmly. I was anything but calm. I know my voice shook, but perhaps it wasn't noticed because of the gruff way in which I spoke. I wasn't even aware of my surroundings on the way back, my mind was whirling so fast.

It was easy! And surely I will be less nervous next time? For there will be a next time. I shall not go tonight because it is Sunday. It would be wrong to commit a crime on a Sunday.

Last night's haul was eleven shillings, a watch that doesn't, of course, mark the time properly, and a silver toothpick in a little silver case. There was also a large quantity of half-eaten sausage. I know who'd eaten it because some of it was still stuck to the toothpick.

This little lot (apart from the sausage) would easily get me to Bristol, but it would hardly take me to America.

August 5th

Bid and Ned insist that I must wait by a different road each time I go out, or at least a different part of the road.

"If you rob in a partickler place, sooner or later someone's going to bring the constable to catch you," said Ned. "I hear them talking in the Stag's Head about things like that. You have to be careful."

"'Tis true," said Bid. "And Susannah, if you're caught, you do know what it means, don't you?"

I could not bring myself to speak. I almost stopped breathing. For so long, I've put it out of my mind – that dreadful sight at the crossroads where I parted from Dominic.

Ned spoke for me. "'Scuse me saying it, Susannah, but you got to know what you're risking. If you're caught, they'll hang you. And you might be strung up and left for the birds to—"

I leapt up. "Hold your tongue, Ned! I will not listen. I do this for my brother, and if I must take risks, I must!"

We were saved from further bad words and worse thoughts by Jack, letting us know that Juliana was riding past.

I looked out of the window. She raised her whip and dipped her head in her own form of a friendly greeting.

I'll show you, Juliana, I thought. One day.

Later

I notice my two friends are at last doing as I asked. They call me by my given name. I am glad they feel close enough to me to be able to do so, but I feel they only find it easy now that I have sunk so low. And that makes me sad.

August 6th

Last night I had such a haul! All because the stupid man shivered like a jelly and practically offered me everything he had. I was confident enough to ride up to him, and snatch whatever he held out to me. He blurted out things like, "Please let me be," and "Take what you want, but spare me," and "Here, here's gold." There was not much gold, but just before I waved my pistol to tell him to go, something made me ask for his gloves. And underneath his gloves were three magnificent rings! He really blubbered when I demanded those. They were family heirlooms, his father would be in a rage when he found out, and so on. I did not care one jot. All I could see was that these would help me and Dominic. I took them. After all, the man did at least have a family, and rings could be replaced. I could not replace my brother if he were to… I cannot write the word.

"Go!" I said to my quaking victim. "You will find other riches in life." I thought that was rather a nice thing to say – sort of the opposite of a curse.

Ned says he'll take the rings to the Stag's Head and ask Sykes MacPhee's advice about who can help him sell them. Oh, I am so excited. They will bring lots and lots of money. Maybe enough for me to leave now!

Today I do not feel good about the man I robbed. But I suppose that's the price I must pay for getting what I need.

I shall not go out this evening. Ned has walked to the Stag's Head, and if the rings fetch enough money, maybe I shan't even need to go out again. Besides, I am tired. Highway robbing is exhausting. All that waiting around wears me out.

But it is exciting!

August 7th

Thank goodness I did not go out robbing last evening. I had a visitation from the de Gracy family as they left for a musical evening at Sir Staveney's home. They were dressed in their best – I have never seen such a quantity of lace and frills and ribbons – but the ladies' fashions are not new. They cannot have the wealth they appeared to have when I first arrived. Maybe I was asking too much when I wanted a loan from them. No! Ridiculous! By their own standards they may not be wealthy any more, but by mine they are rich indeed.

I put Jack outside, of course, so that sweet Juliana wouldn't have reason to throw a fit of the vapours, and they entered. The ladies' eyes were everywhere, and I hoped that Ned had left no traces of his presence. He's normally very good at keeping everything upstairs.

"We wished to greet you, cousin, as we passed," said Sir Roger. (You mean the ladies wanted to show off their finery, I thought.) Then he paused. "What is *that*?"

"That" was a badger's skull from the keeper's collection, that Ned has taken a fancy to. I can't imagine what he wants it for. Juliana leapt back in horror when she saw it. I picked it up. "I'm working on my drawing skills," I said. "This is my model." I congratulated myself on my quick thinking.

"Ugh," said Juliana, so I kept hold of the skull.

The ladies' skirts were so full, and all their hats so well-plumed, they almost filled my little parlour. In fact, I was quite unable to find Bid to ask her to fetch refreshments. Fortunately, these were refused as soon as mentioned.

"It is Lady Vean's birthday," explained Lady Anne. "We are invited."

I hadn't realized there even was a Lady Vean, and said so. Heavens, how much anguish it would have saved me if I'd known that Sir Staveney was already married.

"Goodness, yes," said Juliana. "They have quite a household. Many, many servants, and Dunby, of course, and his child."

Lady Anne smiled. "Dear Dunby."

Juliana flushed and lowered her head. Merciful heaven, are things that bad? Are they going to marry Juliana to the fool? For his money? Surely not.

But it would be the solution. Sir Staveney would gain what his family lacks – good social connections – and Sir Roger would gain what his lacks – money.

When Jack barked suddenly, my heart sank. Ned! Ned was back from the Stag's Head. My insides panicked, while I tried to remain cool on the outside. Fortunately, a flurry in the corner and the door opening and closing told me that Bid had slipped out to warn him.

Juliana was performing as usual. "The beastly dog, Mama, it is coming. Oh, I feel faint…"

"Hush, sweet one," said her mother. "It's outside. And have a care for your hair," she said as Juliana's knees buckled. "Do *try* to stay upright." She turned to me. "You look flustered, cousin. Have you a guest arriving?"

"I… I…" A brilliant inspiration struck me. "To tell you the truth it is no guest you hear," I said.

"But your dog sounds excited. Someone must be here."

"'Tis only the keeper. Did you not see Bid run? Oh, she is *so* frightened of the keeper."

As I prattled on, those around me fell silent. It was as if the air had been sucked out of the room. Then they all spoke together.

"The *keeper*?" That was Sir Roger.

"The *ghost*!" moaned Lady Anne.

Dear sweet Juliana was as white as snow and gibbered quietly to herself. Then she gathered her wits and screeched, "Fathergetmeoutofhere!"

He did not need telling twice. They were all gone with the speed of hunted rats. A lot they cared about me! Nobody thought to save me from the ghost!

I watched the carriage depart, then signalled to my two friends, cowering behind Moonbeam's stable, that it was safe to come in.

"Wherever was they off to?" asked Ned as he limped in.

His poor leg had suffered from the long walk. He is little used to exercise these days, being always cooped up.

"A jolly evening at Sir Staveney's, listening to Madam Juliana playing the virginals," said Bid, putting a jug of ale in front of him. "Drink up. You'll have more fun here."

Ned was thirsty and drained half the jug before realizing Bid had put a cup out for him to use. He glanced at her and laughed. She ruffled his head.

"Must be quite a gathering they'm going to," said Ned. "They was in an 'ell of a hurry, begging your pardon, Susannah."

"It wasn't the gathering that made them run," I said. "It was the keeper."

Bid squealed and moved closer to Ned.

"Not really, Bid," I said. Honestly, that girl can be so dense. "It was Ned who startled Jack. Ned!" I turned to him, and I know excitement must have shown on my face. "How much have we got? Show me!"

He hesitated, then placed two handfuls of coins on the table. I stared in disbelief. "This is all? Ned, please tell me there is more."

He shook his head. "That's all I could get."

"But those rings were worth far more!" I cried. "This—" I scooped up the coins and let them fall through my fingers like giant grains of sand. "This would scarcely pay for a few nights' lodgings while I wait for a ship. Get them back."

Ned gaped at me. "What?"

"You heard me. Get the rings back. I will sell them myself." I fetched my cloak. "Come, Bid. It will be light for a while yet."

But Ned had hold of her hand. "Susannah, I don't care what happens to me, but I will not let you and Bid set foot in the Stag's Head."

Bid nodded. "He's right, my love. We can't let you do it. You put yourself in danger enough most evenings. Now give me your cloak, sit down, and I'll make you a warm posset, calm your nerves."

I did as she said. It was only at that point that I realized Bid is older than me. I am no longer the mistress and she the servant. She has begun to mother me. What a sweet girl – woman – she is.

Ned explained the rules of fencing. The person you sell stolen goods to is called a fence. He gives you a much lower price than you'd get if you sold the goods yourself. "The fence, see," said Ned, "has double danger, 'cos he might get caught with the stolen goods, and when he takes them to sell he lays himself open to robbery or to being caught. And he knows the best place to sell stolen things, which people like you and me don't. Very valuable, is fences."

He *has* learned a lot. But so have I. I've learned to be brave and strong. It's obvious that the bits and pieces I rob from walkers and the odd rider are going to amount to only a little.

I must be even braver and hold up someone more likely to yield a good haul.

Ned and Bid drank more ale than they should and I had two cups of strong wine. When Ned said, "Why don't we all go out and hold up the de Gracy carriage on its way back?" we laughed.

"Ooh, yes! It would be easy," I said, and Bid and I got quite giggly about what we'd do to Juliana. Then Ned spoiled it all by getting serious and saying he'd tie us down before he'd let us do anything so foolhardy.

But it made me think of the pickings that could be had. A carriage! That's my next target. But not just yet.

August 12th

Three nights out (not Sunday, of course) and I collected a small haul of money and rings, and a beautiful gold and silver necklace that some young lover was taking to his lady. He begged me to return it, but I have to harden my heart against such pleas. My need is greater. He can buy another necklace. If I lost Dominic, I could never have another brother.

Ned is storing everything for me. We think – at least I think – it might be better to take the jewellery and a fancy carved walnut case, containing a silver watch, to the city, to sell ourselves. I am excited. My wealth is building slowly. Just a little more luck and there will be enough. Then I can forget my life of crime and concentrate on the good I can do. Must do.

Tonight I shall try the road I came in on when I first arrived at Gracy Park. I do not remember the driver hurrying at all. Perhaps, because it doesn't lead to a city, people are not so afraid to travel along it.

August 13th

I did it! I held up a carriage! I have collected so much! My only sadness is that I did not have another horse, or I could have carried more.

Oh, it was so easy. I let three single riders and a pair of fat churchmen pass by. They little knew the danger that lurked in the trees along the road. Oh, who am I fooling! They'd be in no danger from me, with my empty gun and my girl's strength. But they would fear me!

When the carriage appeared, I moved out in front of it. That's always a dangerous moment. The driver could be brave enough to whip the horses up and drive straight at me.

But not this one. He pulled them to a halt and said, "I've got nothing, my friend." He jerked a thumb over his shoulder. "Try them inside."

"Get down," I said. "Sit on the roadside and don't move, or you're dead."

He shrugged. "Don't worry. I ain't moving."

I urged Moonbeam forward and banged on the side of the carriage with my pistol. "Them inside" stuck their heads out, and had obviously been asleep.

"What? What?" said a plump red-faced man.

"Eh? *Eh*?" The well-dressed, untidy woman opposite him looked bemused for a moment, then she saw my pistol and screamed. "Help! Murder!"

I wanted to slap her face to shut her up, but instead I ordered, in my deepest voice. "Hold! Be still and no harm will come to you."

Instead of being still, she turned to her husband and began to rant at him. "I TOLD you we should have stopped at that inn. I TOLD you. But no, we'll push on, you said, we'll be there before dark, and no, it's a quiet road, you said, there's no danger and NOW look at us. All our worldly goods are in this carriage and we're about to lose them. You FOOL!"

"Quiet!" her husband and I said together.

"I will not take all," I said. "I want your silver plate, your jewels and your money."

Well, there followed such an argument that I was afraid

the whole world might hear. I almost turned to go, but I was tempted by those words, "all our worldly goods".

The man got out and I tossed him my sack. "Fill it," I ordered. "Start with those rings and that pearl necklace your wife is trying to hide beneath her gorget." I had seen her hands fluttering at her throat, and I would *adore* to own some pearls.

Once the jewels were in, I said, "Your money."

He reached into the carriage and pulled out a small leather pouch. "In," I said, gesturing with the pistol towards the sack.

He obeyed. "That's it."

Something told me he was lying. "When I said your money, I meant all of it," I growled. At least, I tried to growl, but my voice cracked and simply sounded hoarse and harsh. But it was enough. With his wife berating him at every move, he reached beneath her skirts and pulled out a small chest, about the size of a loaf of bread.

"Take it, you scab!" he snarled.

"The sack," I said. He put it inside. "And there's room for more – your silver."

His wife was wailing now, and threatening him with fifty different kinds of vengeance when she got him to their new home, but I didn't care. I saw a set of silver goblets go into the sack, and a small salver.

Suddenly, my courage left me. I'd been there too long.

I needed to get away before someone came. Reaching down, I took the sack from him and, with difficulty, swung it up in front of me.

"You may keep the rest, with the highwayman's blessing," I said.

Obviously very relieved they weren't to lose everything they owned, they thanked me. It made me feel so – I don't know – so bountiful. I liked the feeling.

I know for sure that when I'm with Dominic and our lives run smoothly, I will do good. I know I will.

Later

All day I've hugged the knowledge to myself that I now have a lot of valuable goods. I am sure that when everything's sold there'll be enough to get me to America and to help me start a new life with Dominic. Just one more hold-up, then maybe I'll even have enough to employ a servant to help us grow things and build things – at least until my brother is completely well and strong.

Yes, just one more hold-up, tonight – then I'll give up my life of crime.

Poor Godfrey had to settle for a walk with me and Jack

today. I was so restless I felt unable to teach him a word. I am so close to being ready to go to Dominic. I *need* to leave.

I've scarcely given the actual journey a thought. Getting to Bristol will be easy. I shall ride Moonbeam – both of us with clean noses! I am experienced now in using inns, so that holds no fear for me. How long will the sea voyage take? Two months? Please God that Dominic will not be taken by his illness. Once I am there, I know all will be well. Just hold on, Dominic. And Hannah Carew, please be kind and generous a little longer. I will repay you.

August 14th

Yesterday evening felt so long, though the road was busy. I let several people go past my hiding place at the edge of a wood. One group of three were drunk; the tallest and drunkest was sick on the road. His friends put their arms round him to help him along. The thought of touching anything belonging to that disgusting trio quite put me off robbing them. I wanted to come out of the shadows and tell them how lucky they were, but that would have been foolhardy, and I would have been as much of a show-off as the de Gracy ladies when they were dressed to impress the Vean family.

Eventually I resigned myself to the fact that there was to be no fruitful carriage hold-up and I settled for robbing the first person who came along: man, woman, churchman, on foot, on horseback or even drunk. I couldn't go home empty-handed.

My prey signalled his approach by tuneless whistling. I moved into the middle of the road. "Hold! Your money, sir!"

He stood and stared at me, mouth wide open.

I waved my pistol. "Or your life…?"

He jumped into action and fumbled around his clothing, which looked quite unsavoury. Fishing out a handful of coins, he held them out to me.

I moved forward and took them.

"I hope you hang for taking what little I have," he said. "I hope I see your rotten corpse in yonder gibbet."

I turned to look in the direction in which he nodded. My face, behind my mask, must have paled at the sight. A gibbet, its ghastly load swaying in the wind, topped the next hill.

My mouth dried, and my heart pounded. Courage, Susannah, I told myself. Looking at the coins the man held out, I whispered hoarsely, "'Tis all you have?"

"Aye. All the money I have in the world," he muttered, "but at home I have a wife and three little 'uns to feed. Go on, then, take it, damn yer eyes."

I could not. I was shuddering inside, and almost unable to speak. I cleared my throat and said, "Keep it. Feed your children. Go."

He slowly closed his fingers over the coins, but he continued to stare at me. I waved him on with my pistol. As he passed, he looked directly into my eyes and said, "A mother yourself, are you?"

Stupid, stupid Susannah. I was so overcome with emotion I had spoken in my normal voice.

"GO!" I shouted and, pulling Moonbeam's head around, I went through the trees and on to open land, where I galloped away, not looking where I was going. Only now I am safe in Keeper's Cottage do I realize how dangerous that was. Moonbeam could have stumbled and thrown me, and I'd have been discovered wearing my mask and men's clothes.

This morning I feel better. I must go out again tonight, perhaps where I took the last carriage. I must. I failed last night. This will be the last time, whether I am successful or not. I shall have to make do with the hoard Ned is keeping for me.

Late at night

Oh, so much to write, and it may be my last chance. This is also my last theft. I have taken paper from a dead woman's table, and used her ink. I shall have to leave my writings here, or perhaps I'll stuff it all inside my clothes and take it to … to wherever I next find myself.

Where shall I begin? With the normal doings of the day? A game with Jack, dinner with Ned and Bid, a chat about how much we'll all miss each other when I go to America? Our hopes and dreams for a joyful reunion when Dominic and I return?

I cannot sleep, not here in this strange bedchamber, but I do not know what time of night it is, and I may not have long before…

I cannot bring myself to write the words. I shall simply say what happened.

I was on the top road – at the very place where I made my first attempt at robbing. I was masked, with pistol at the ready. It was a still evening. Down in the valley to the right I could just make out the lights of the Stag's Head. Mist pooled and swirled round the main building, and I could see nothing of those two silver ribbons of water that I'd seen before, no, not even the bridges.

As I'd wished and longed for, I heard wheels rattling along the road. The way was rutted, and the driver shouted at his horses to hold steady, keep pulling.

A carriage appeared around a bend. It had a riderless horse tied on, still saddled. The rider, I reasoned, must be taking a break in the carriage, which suited me admirably.

I surprised myself at my confidence. Just a while ago, I

was afraid to tackle a carriage, but it actually seemed easy – easier than a man on horseback.

I pushed Moonbeam on, into the middle of the way. There was no need for me to shout, "Hold!" The driver, who looked exhausted, pulled the horses up immediately. They'd hardly been making any speed over the rough ground anyway.

"You! Get down," I growled. The driver practically fell off in his haste to do as I said. I moved to the window, and – well, it all happened so fast. A woman looked out, screamed and shrieked, "Wake up! Quick! We're attacked!" and the man behind her stirred and looked at me.

It was Sir Staveney Vean!

He roared in fury. I should have made as if to fire my pistol, but I panicked. I was sure he'd recognize me. I yanked poor Moonbeam's head round and galloped off downhill as fast as I could, not caring where I went. Some instinct told me to keep off de Gracy lands, but otherwise I rode blindly. As I reached a dip where the road rose steeply before dropping down into the valley I glanced round. He was behind me. I cursed. That horse, still saddled. Oh why had I ever thought it was easy?

Sir Staveney roared again and I heard a shot. Of course he'd be armed. I cannot say what terror seized my heart when clouds masked the moon. All chance of escaping across country was lost if I, and particularly Moonbeam, could not see.

I had no choice. I knew where I had to go. Shouting encouragement at Moonbeam, I leaned low and we galloped down the track. Branches brushed my hat, and I thanked heaven that I wasn't using a side-saddle, or I might have taken the top of my head off. Even above the noise we made, I heard Sir Staveney's curses, and the steady pounding of his horse's hooves.

There! At the end, where the track curved to the left, there was the Stag's Head. If what Ned told me about it was true, I felt that I – a criminal – would find help there.

Faster, faster, skidding round the corner into the inn yard. A burly man rolling a barrel. He looked up in surprise. Sykes MacPhee? It must be.

"Help me!" I cried. "I'm in fear of my life!"

Sykes MacPhee motioned me behind an outhouse. I hunched low in the saddle as Moonbeam and I fought to catch our breath.

I listened. I could hear the other horse coming nearer. At the same time, I became aware of the shadowy figures of men moving around behind me. There were murmurs. I caught one: "'Tis a wench."

My hat had come off, and my hair was loose! If I escaped Sir Staveney, I knew there'd be fresh dangers to fear.

But now my attention was on the sound of the horse that clattered into the yard.

"Out of my way, MacPhee!"

There was a sharp cry of pain, then Sir Staveney's voice

again. "I said out of my *way*! If you're harbouring a damned highwayman, I'll see you swing. Stand aside!"

Another cry of pain. I could expect no protection here. Once more I panicked. Kicking wildly, I urged Moonbeam to a gallop, off down a side track to where I saw the gleam of water. We crossed the first bridge and I pulled Moonbeam left, to head down the raised path between the river and the stream. But the poor exhausted horse couldn't make the turn. He plunged into the water and I flew off his back. Good luck and ill luck were with me. Good luck that it was the shallower stream rather than the faster-flowing river, but bad luck that there was little water to break my fall. I was stunned.

My next memory is of being dragged to the carriage, which must have followed Sir Staveney to the Stag's Head. No one gathered round this time. They all kept well back in the shadows.

The last I saw, before I passed out, was Moonbeam being led into a stable by Sykes MacPhee.

I came to, to find my hands and feet tied, and Lady Staveney sitting bug-eyed, staring at me. There was a small girl in the carriage, too – Elvina? – but, fortunately, no Dunby. I could not have borne him seeing me like this. Seeing the child shocked me. I can't believe I would have robbed a little one. I smiled at her, to calm her fear, though it can't have been greater than mine. Her little pinched face looked coldly back. It is not a loving household, this one.

Sir Staveney rode alongside, pistol at the ready. I wondered where we were going. Not for long. We drew up at what I could only imagine, by its grandness, to be the Vean home.

"You can't bring her in the house, husband," whimpered Lady Vean.

"It's late, woman. I'm not going to do anything more about it tonight. I'll keep her under lock and key, and she can be dealt with tomorrow by the justice of the peace."

"What will happen to her, Grandfather?" asked the little girl as he lifted her down, not too gently.

"The sheriff will put her in gaol, then she'll be taken to court and judgement will be passed."

"What does that mean, Grandfather?"

"She'll hang."

At these words, terror overtook me and I struggled against my bonds. It was futile, and I soon collapsed in a sobbing heap. I remember begging Lady Vean to make her husband spare me, but she looked at me icily, stepped carefully over my sodden boots and was helped down from the carriage.

So here I am, locked in a gloomy bedchamber. It is well furnished, with tapestry hangings, a large bed, a closet full of women's clothes, and a close-stool, so I have no need of a chamber pot. There is a carved table with tiny painted dishes, for cosmetics, I suppose, and a pretty ivory comb. It also holds a dressing-box, which I have not opened, and there is a pen, some ink and a supply of paper, all of which I am using. I am convinced no one will notice, because I believe that this is the bedchamber of Dunby Vean's poor dead wife. Oh, perhaps it is used occasionally for guests, but it has the feel of a room gone cold.

There is no escape from the window – it's a sheer drop and at best I would break my legs. I thought I might tie the bed coverings into a rope and escape by lowering myself down the wall, but it is too far. I would have too dangerous a jump to the ground.

The key is in the door – I can see it when I look through the keyhole – and I hear someone outside, snoring deeply. They have posted a guard. I have a stump of candle, set in a bowl of water. How I should like to take the candle and set the bed hangings on fire. The only thing that stops me is the thought of the danger to that innocent child.

Later

I cannot sleep. I shiver with fear. I am to die, I know it. Sir Staveney will show no mercy. He knows my de Gracy relations will be glad to be rid of me, once they know I am a common criminal who would bring shame on them. And he himself hates me because I rejected his son. Well, his son will get what he deserves – Juliana. She will fit well with this mean, cold family.

But I ... I will die. And what will become of poor Dominic? Who will help him then? I have let him down and I cannot bear it.

Oh, how cruel life is. Just when I have enough to get me to the ship, and probably to secure a berth on board, just then everything turns sour. Poor Ned, poor Bid. They'll be wondering what's happened to me. Though Bid will hear soon enough when news gets round Gracy Park.

I am so afraid. Afraid of the rope. And the gibbet...

Days later

That night! That dreadful, soul-destroying, fearsome night!

I was wakeful. When I saw a glimmer of light in the sky, I knew I would sleep no more.

And then the smell. Smoke! But my candle had gone out long ago.

The smoky smell grew stronger. It wasn't the smell of cooking, or of a good log burning. It was a bad smell.

Fire!

The house was on fire! As I ran to bang on the door, there

were shouts from below, and the sound of feet running – away! Thank the Lord, I thought, the fire has been discovered. But as minutes passed, and the shouts grew louder and more terrified, and the smell grew worse, I realized I was forgotten.

I hammered on the door with my fists. Hammered and hammered. Then I picked up the poker from the fireplace and beat upon the door with that. Surely the guard would come back and let me out? Was I forgotten in the panic downstairs?

I heard crashes and screams. People calling each other.

I wept, sobbed, and threw myself at the door with all my might.

"Don't let me burn!" I screamed and, finding strength I never knew I had, I threw myself again at the door. This time, the lock gave – I felt it give! With a fresh burst of energy and hope, I hurled myself twice more at the door. It burst open! I tumbled through into a corridor. I could see stairs at the end, but clouds of smoke billowed upwards from below. The noise of crashing and roaring and breaking glass was louder now. I hurtled down the first flight of stairs, but could go no further. Flames licked at the next landing, and the smoke churning upwards was dense and black and choking.

There were two ways I could go, corridors to left and right. I chose left – the air looked clearer there.

I ran to a window at the end and flung it open. There was a drop down on to a flat, roofed area. I remembered my idea of tying bedding together, and darted into the nearest room. I grabbed the sheets and coverlet from a bed and tied them together in big clumsy knots. Knowing how knots in washing would never come undone if they were wet, I looked around. There! A jug and bowl, and mercifully the jug was full. I poured water over my knots. Back in the corridor, I dragged a chest to the window. It had iron handles on each side. I tied my rope of sheets to one handle, and climbed on to the sill.

As I gripped the sheets and swung myself over, I gasped as I dropped suddenly, then stopped. The chest must have pulled up against the window. Slowly, my heart thumping, and terrified to open my eyes, I began my downward climb. There was no one below, and I began to think I might get down and away before I was spotted. Everyone was at the front of the house. I imagined the scene. Family, servants and animals running round in confusion, buckets of water…

I looked down to check how far it was to the temporary safety of the flat roof and, as I did so, I heard thin screams from above. Glancing up, I saw, to my horror, the pale, pinched, terrified face of the little girl from the carriage – Elvina. And behind her, the angry tips of flames darted amid the smoke.

What should I do? If I dropped down now, and lowered myself from the flat roof, I could get away, I could. To go back, to help the child, meant time lost and probable discovery. I would hang, for sure.

They'd left me to die in the flames. They had. I should leave the whole lot of them and save myself.

But I could not do it. My shoulders shrieked with the pain of holding on, but I climbed up, back up the rope of sheets.

Suddenly, cries and shouts from below told me I'd been seen.

"The child!" shouted a man "She's still inside!"

"Save her!" cried a woman's voice. "Oh, save her, please!" She began to cry hysterically.

At least, if I could rescue the child, there would be help for the last part of our descent. I reached the sill. "Help me up," I cried, but the child just grabbed me, crying, her fingers digging into my arm and neck.

"Quiet!" I snapped. "Help me up, and I will carry you down." How I would do that I wasn't quite sure.

My harsh words jerked her out of her shock. She pulled and I strained, and soon I was back on the landing. My legs and arms trembled uncontrollably. I took off my belt – Dominic's belt – and bound her to me, her face to my chest.

"Don't be afraid," I said. "Just hold on with all your strength."

I lowered myself more carefully this time, but our combined weight was too much for my aching, strained arms. My hands lost their tight grip on the sheets, and slipped, taking us ever faster, down towards the flat roof. I closed my eyes, waiting for the pain of landing.

But there was no pain. Strong hands grasped us and lowered us down. Then the child was taken from me by two men who had climbed on to the roof, and she was passed down into other stretching arms, and to safety.

Then it was my turn, and I was lowered down with just as much care. When I reached the ground, I crumpled, crawled away from the building and was violently and painfully sick.

A servant woman helped me up. She smelled of milk and cheese. I saw Sir Staveney looking down at me.

"Take her to the lodge," he said. "Guard the door."

A stable boy carried me to a cottage, where a plump, kindly woman gave me strong drink. It was harsh on my throat, but warmed my blood.

"You'm a brave girl," she said. "The child would have died else."

"How did she get left behind?" I asked.

"Too many nursery maids," said the woman. "Each thought one of the others had her safe, but no one had her at all, poor mite. They'll be in trouble, that's for sure."

She patted my head and left me alone. I heard voices outside the room and a key turned in the lock.

I hurt so badly. My arms and shoulders felt stretched and strained, and my back was sore. I curled up in a corner and breathed deeply, trying to clear the smoke from my lungs, but all I did was cough.

And then Sir Staveney stood before me again.

"For the crimes you committed," he said, "you deserve to hang."

I put my head down and began to weep, silently.

"But I cannot forget," he continued, "that you could have saved yourself, but you chose to save my son's child."

Days later

So here I am. The air is clean and fresh, with the tang of salt, and it is so *good* to be alive.

Sir Staveney freed me. Well, not exactly. He sent to Keeper's Cottage for my clothes.

"And search the place," he ordered his men. "Bring back everything she stole."

At least Bid and Ned will know what's happened to me, that I have not deserted them willingly.

When my clothes arrived, Sir Staveney flung them at me. "Get dressed. At least *go* like a lady."

His final words to me. He still despises me.

I was brought here, to this ship. The cost of my passage is Sir Staveney's gift to me, in exchange for his grandchild's life. I am in the care, and under the watchful eye, of the ship's master. And on tomorrow's tide we are bound for America!

And so I leave England. I have some regrets. My darling Jack. It breaks my heart to know I'll never see him again, the poor little soul. I couldn't say farewell to Ned and Bid. I couldn't bring Moonbeam. And all the money and silver and jewels we'd put away will have been taken by Sir Staveney's men. I suppose they'll have taken Moonbeam, too.

Perhaps Bid will look after Jack. I shall never know.

The breeze is strong. It plays tricks on me. I keep hearing my name. Perhaps it's blowing on a breeze from America. Perhaps it is Dominic calling me.

I'm coming, Dominic!

Later

Yes, Dominic, I'm coming! But not alone! I *did* hear my name on the breeze. And when I heard it more clearly, I looked ashore and who did I see? Moonbeam! And riding him were Ned and Bid.

As if that wasn't wonderful enough, when I called out to them, a white bundle in Bid's arms started to wriggle. Jack!

What a joyous reunion!

"We couldn't let you go alone, Susannah," said Ned. "Soon as we heard you'd been saved from the hangman's noose, my Bid went up to the house to find out what was happening to you."

My Bid, eh? I smiled. "You say you're coming with me?

I suppose we could sell Moonbeam to pay for your passage, but will it be enough for both of you?"

Bid laughed aloud. "Susannah, we have plenty! Sykes MacPhee sent a man to tell us about your capture. Ned hid your money and jewels and things in such clever places, Sir Staveney's lackeys didn't find a thing!"

My clever, clever friends.

"I hid some of it in the badger's skull," said Ned, "and some in Jack's bed. He growled at them, and they didn't bother him no more. And the rest I bundled in rags in among the keeper's rubbish."

"And when they started to poke about in it," Bid continued, "I said 'Be careful, that lot's been there since the plague.' Didn't they move!"

And so, with money in hand, I go at last to my brother. Ned and Bid will settle down with us in the new land and, between us, there's nothing we can't do. We'll look after Moonbeam until Dominic is strong again. And if he doesn't get strong I will take care of us all. After all, I've learned to garden, I can teach French, and I can cook (with help). I can also ride like a man, and if we are ever truly desperate I could always…

No! I mustn't let those thoughts into my mind. Not ever again.

Historical note

Thieves have always been ready to steal from travellers for as long as there have been tracks from place to place. In medieval times, huge robber gangs terrorized some areas, and whole stretches of forest were cut back from the roadside so that there were fewer places for robbers to lurk. Along what's now the A31 road near Alton in Hampshire, hundreds of members of a gang had to be rounded up and hanged before travellers could feel even remotely safe.

Roads around London were especially dangerous, as were country roads along which wealthy people travelled, such as those to Bath and Dover. The roads were quiet, with few buildings along the way, and it was all too easy for a highwayman to commit his crime and disappear into the well-wooded countryside.

Travellers did their best not to turn themselves into tempting prospects for a robber. They would disguise themselves as poor people, or band together to travel in a convoy. Many armed themselves; some had a small amount of cash ready to hand to the highwayman, while they hid the rest in secret pockets and other – they hoped – ingenious places.

The highwayman was the lone masked stranger on horseback, brandishing a pistol and stepping menacingly out in front of his victim. The age when most of these daring robbers flourished was from about 1640 to 1800. The English Civil War produced a number of desperate ex-soldiers who turned to this form of crime to make a living, often loyally robbing only members of the opposite side; thus a Royalist would only rob a Roundhead and vice versa.

The punishment for highway robbery was death, and the hanging of a highwayman, particularly a notorious one, was a popular public event. Many captured highwaymen spent their last days in London's Newgate Prison, which was filthy and stank horribly. The prison's water supply was polluted by a cesspool, and the building was crawling with vermin, so disease was rife.

Those highwaymen who were simply hanged were the lucky ones. Some, like Royalist James Hind, were hanged, drawn and quartered. This punishment usually meant that the victim was cut down from the noose while still alive, then had his insides removed and burned in front of him. Finally his body was cut into quarters. The four bits were preserved, then displayed in four different places, as an awful warning to others.

The body of highwayman Jerry Abershaw, who decorated his prison walls with pictures of his exploits, was hung in a metal cage known as a gibbet. Again, this was to be a warning to others, and his corpse was visited by hundreds of sightseers. There are records of men who were put in the gibbet while still alive, where they hung for days in agony until they died and rotted.

But these hideous punishments weren't enough to put many men off turning to highway robbery. Or women! Moll Cutpurse (real name, Mary Frith) was a tomboy and teenage rebel who began her criminal career as a pickpocket. She became a pipe-smoking fence who sold the goods other thieves had stolen, in her shop in London's Fleet Street. It's said that she became so well known that people who'd been robbed would go to her shop to buy back their own possessions! Moll caught the public imagination, and many stories sprang up around her. It's said that she once robbed a famous general, and galloped away with the loot. Unfortunately for her, she rode her horse so hard it collapsed, exhausted, and she was caught and imprisoned. But by then Moll was so wealthy she was able to pay up the sum of £2,000, which saved her from the rope. In today's terms, she'd probably have to pay a hundred times that amount!

Not all highwaymen or women were so unusual or eccentric. When William Davis was captured, people who knew him were astounded. By day he was a farmer but, at the drop of a hat, he'd don a disguise and go off highway-robbing. His disguises were so good that he once robbed his landlord of 70 guineas that he, Davis, had paid him in rent just an hour or so before! He became known as the Golden Farmer, because he always paid his debts in gold, and he met his end dangling from a noose.

Some highwaymen, like Frenchman Claude Duval, became glamorous figures of legend, but even the pleas of lady admirers failed to save them from execution.

The end of the road came for highwaymen with better policing, mounted patrols and toll roads, which had manned gates. Their legends grew, and ballads and tales of their daring exploits and bravery on the gallows abounded. They're often glamorized in films, plays, opera and books, but the reality was that they were dangerous, often vicious criminals who terrorized the traveller.

Timeline

1642 King Charles I wants to rule without Parliament. Civil wars, between the Cavaliers (Royalists supporting the king) and Oliver Cromwell's Roundheads (supporters of Parliament), begin, and continue until 1649.

1649

Jan 30 Charles I is executed.

Mar 17/19 Parliament abolishes the House of Lords and the monarchy.

May Oliver Cromwell declares Britain is a republic, known as the Commonwealth.

1651

Jan 1 Charles's son is crowned King Charles II at Scone in Scotland.

Sept 3 Charles II is defeated in battle at Worcester, by Cromwell.

Oct Charles escapes to France. He's in exile for the next nine years.

1653

Dec Cromwell becomes Lord Protector. He was invited to become king, but turned the offer down.

1658

Sept 3 Oliver Cromwell dies. His son Richard is named as his successor.

1659

May 25 Richard Cromwell resigns after pressure from the discontented army.

1660

Jan 1 Samuel Pepys begins his famous diary.

May 29 Charles II is restored to the throne. He enters London on his 30th birthday, to general rejoicing.

1662

May 21 Charles II marries the Portuguese princess Catherine of Braganza.

1665 The Great Plague of London kills over 50,000 people.

1666

Sept 2–5 The Great Fire of London destroys hundreds of churches, including St Paul's Cathedral, and makes thousands homeless. Newgate prison is burned.

1669

May 31 Samuel Pepys stops writing his diary, fearing he's losing his sight.

1672 Newgate prison is rebuilt. Conditions are still dreadful.

1675 Sir Christopher Wren begins rebuilding St Paul's Cathedral.

1682 approx Londoners could buy fire insurance for the first time.

1685

Feb 6 Charles II dies, succeeded by his brother, James II.

1832 Gibbeting is abolished.

1861 The death penalty is limited to four crimes: murder, treason, arson in royal dockyards and piracy with violence.

1868 Last public execution.

1902 Newgate prison is demolished. The Central Criminal Court, known as the Old Bailey, stands on the site.

1969 British MPs vote to suspend the death penalty for five years. It is never reintroduced.

Picture acknowledgments

P 164	The Print Collector/Alamy
P 165	Classic Image/Alamy
P 166	Mary Evans Picture Library/Alamy
P 167	Mary Evans Picture Library/Alamy
P 167	Mary Evans Picture Library/GROSVENOR PRINTS
P 168	Mary Evans Picture Library/Alamy
P 169	Cannon/The Kobal Collection
P 170	Museum of London/HIP/TopFoto
P 171	The Board of Trustees of the Armouries/HIP/TopFoto
P 171	c.2000 TopFoto. TopFoto.co.uk

King Charles II's father was publicly beheaded, and Charles himself went on the run after his Cavaliers were beaten by Oliver Cromwell's army. After several years in France and the Netherlands, Charles was restored to the throne in 1660 and reigned for 25 years.

Oliver Cromwell's Roundheads were so successful in battle that Cromwell eventually became Lord Protector of England – its ruler. Eventually, Parliament offered to make him king, but he refused. When he died and his son Richard took over, Parliament lost its power. A new Parliament invited Charles II to come home and rule. The King forgave all his enemies, except those who'd signed his father's death warrant.

When handsome highwayman Claude Duval held up a coach, the wealthy lady inside took out her flageolet – a small flute – and played a few notes. The idea was to show she wasn't scared. The story goes that Claude took out his own flageolet and played too. He then invited the lady to dance and enjoyed himself so much that he finally left with much less cash than he'd normally have demanded.

William Davis, the "Golden Farmer", had an extraordinarily long criminal career, and it's said that in all that time even his wife and children hadn't a clue about his other life. He was quite happy to rob hardworking folk, and this picture shows him robbing one of the poorest of all, a travelling tinker.

James Hind was a Royalist and an ex-soldier, loyal to the king, and many of his victims were Cromwell's men. In this picture he's robbing a Parliamentarian while riders gallop by unaware a crime's being committed. Stories about Hind show that he had a touch of Robin Hood about him and occasionally helped people instead of robbing them.

Moll Cutpurse wore men's clothes even when she wasn't highway-robbing. She smoked a pipe, too! Smoking was popular in her day, because people didn't realize how badly it damaged their health. Even so, proper ladies didn't smoke – at least, not in public.

This still from a film called *The Wicked Lady* shows the beautiful Lady Katherine Ferrers, who was married at sixteen. She hated living at her husband's dull country home and she loathed her husband's sister. When, for sheer excitement, Lady Katherine turned to highway robbery, she was thrilled that her first victim turned out to be her sister-in-law!

A prison stood on the Newgate site for at least 800 years. It had a grim reputation for filth, squalor, ill-treatment and disease.

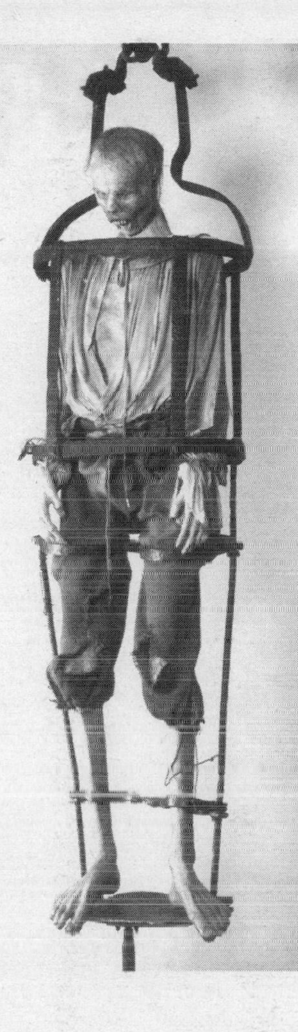

The dummy in this gibbet cage shows museum visitors how a hanged body would be displayed to the public. Sometimes, criminals would be put in the cage while still alive, and allowed to starve or freeze to death. To passers-by, it was a gruesome warning to obey the law.

Gibbets were often set up at crossroads, where many people passed. The cage would be hung from the wooden arm.

Experience history first-hand with My Story –
a series of vividly imagined accounts of life in the past.

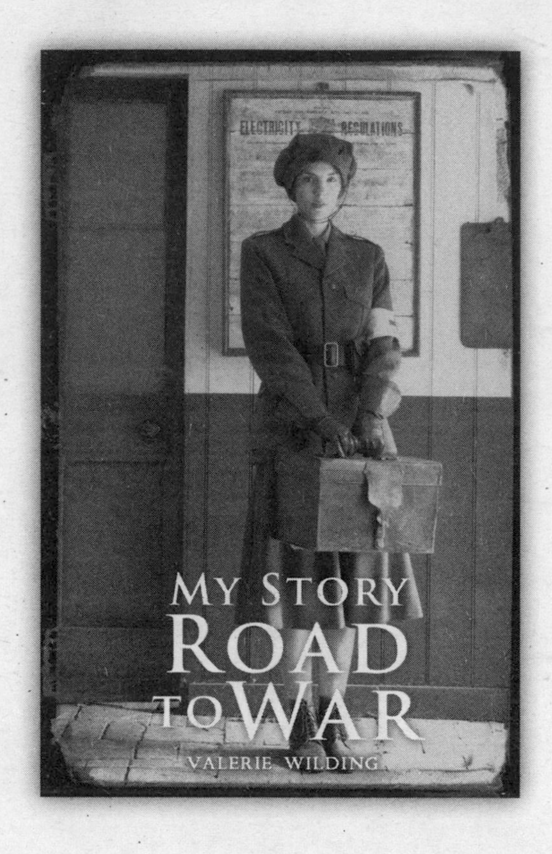
ELECTRICITY REGULATIONS
MY STORY
ROAD
TO WAR
VALERIE WILDING